MAYBE

JOY AVERY

MAYBE

First Print Edition: November 2017

DEDICATION

Dedicated to the dream.

DEAR READER,

As always, THANK YOU for your support of **#joyaveryromance**.

While *Maybe* does touch on a sensitive subject, I pray I've written it in a way that shows a beautiful journey of unconditional love, strength, and devotion. I hope you enjoy Rana and Dallas's tale as much as I've enjoyed penning it.

Please help me spread the word about Maybe by recommending this love story to friends and family, book clubs, social media and online forums. I'd also like to ask that you please take a moment to leave a review on the site where you purchased this novel. Reviews help!

I love hearing from readers. Feel free to email me at: authorjoyavery@gmail.com

Until next time, HAPPY READING!

ACKNOWLEDGMENTS

To everyone who has supported me on this glorious journey, THANK YOU!

1

Rana Lassiter didn't know two people more deserving of happily-ever-after than her younger sister Gadiya and her new husband, Nico. The Duprees. The title brought a smile to Rana's face. They'd been through so much. She was glad they'd finally found their way back to each other.

The power of love. No one could look at those two and not believe in its healing powers. *Love*, she thought. *The one thing with the ability to break and restore you*. Right now, she was in the broken category.

Pushing away the thoughts attempting to creep into her head, she admired the love birds as they slow-danced to Stevie Wonder's "Ribbon in the Sky." The affectionate way Nico eyed his new wife told Rana she had nothing to worry about. Nico would take good care of her sister.

She couldn't help but beam at them. God, they made such a beautiful couple. She wanted that. *One day*, she told herself. *But for right now, I'm focused on me*.

Rana's gaze slid past the newlyweds and landed on a sight just as spectacular. *Dallas Fontaine.* Mount Pleasance, North Carolina's newest arrival. The name rang in Rana's head like a sexy melody of dominance and power. And that was exactly what the six-two, dark brown skin, fit and toned man exuded.

Rana tried to ignore him, but her body acted as a conduit for all of the sex appeal dripping from him. If she thought she could handle being meshed up against his solid frame, she would have asked him to dance.

She recalled their initial introduction and the burst of electricity that had shot up her arm when they'd shaken hands. Yeah, staying away from him was probably the right decision. That kind of jolt suggested any interaction with him was a bad idea.

Dallas stood chatting with several other reception attendees. The expensive black suit he wore fit him as one did a mannequin in the window of a designer boutique. Lord, the sinful things she could imagine doing with him. Too bad she was on a dating hiatus. A man hiatus was more like it.

As if he'd sensed her naughty thoughts, he glanced in her direction, causing heat to pool in her belly. A woman had to appreciate a man who could ignite her body without a single touch. Yeah, it'd been far too long since she'd experienced the intimate rousing of a man.

Maybe she could make a one-time exception to her man hiatus. She couldn't give him forever, but one night wasn't sounding too bad. Rana laughed at herself. At thirty-four, she'd outgrown one-night stands. Plus, they'd never really been her thing. However, in this case...

Dallas's presence was like lightning; it did little damage until it struck. And he struck. Struck hard, hammering her system unlike anything she'd ever experienced before. He flashed a relaxed smile that glowed with several watts of intense brilliance. When he winked, her insides shimmed.

Too, too bad.

"Careful, baby sis. Someone might get zapped by all of the sparks you two are setting off."

Rana dragged her attention away from admiring Dallas and toward the eldest Lassiter sister, Sadona. As always, the radiant beauty was flawless. From the perfectly applied make-up, to the neat off-set bun she wore low on the back of her head. The lilac matron-of-honor dress accented those Lassiter curves they'd all been blessed with.

"A fireman should know better than to play with matches," Rana said.

The inferno Dallas had lit inside of her still burned ferociously, melting her from the inside out. She struggled not to toss a desire-filled glance in his direction.

Sadona crossed her arms over her chest and

eyed Gadiya and Nico locked in a tight embrace. "Those two were meant for each other."

Rana noted the hint of sadness in Sadona's voice. "Hey, sis. I've been meaning to ask you...is everything okay? With you and Alec, I mean."

Rana didn't like meddling in either of her sister's personal lives, but it was obvious that something was wrong with Sadona. She hadn't been herself since she'd arrived in Mount Pleasance over a week and a half ago. Plus, Alec hadn't bothered to attend the wedding. He'd always treated Gadiya like the little sister he'd never had. And to miss her wedding... Yep, something was up.

Sadona flashed what Rana perceived as a forced smile. Her sister had never been good at hiding her emotions. There was definitely trouble in paradise, and Rana wanted to know what kind. Maybe they were experiencing the seven-year-itch phenomenon. At least she hoped that was all it was.

"We'll talk later. Tonight is about nothing but love and happiness," Sadona said.

Sadona's choice of words told Rana everything she needed to know. She nodded slowly, "Okay. But later, we talk."

Sensing the caress of dark, daunting eyes on her, Rana slid her gaze back in Dallas's direction. Sure enough, his eyes were pinned firmly to her. He wasn't smiling, wasn't frowning, just observing. His thumb moved back and forth against the rim of the glass he held as if he were in deep thought. She would pay a fortune to know what was racing through his mind. By the glint in his brown eyes, his thoughts were as impure as hers.

It was nice to know she still had it. Even if she had no plans of using any of it.

Just when she thought her body would suffer a lust-induced meltdown, the wedding planner saved her, announcing for all the single woman to gather in the center of the room. Single, but content, definitely described her current situation.

Freeing herself from the confines of Dallas's intense scrutiny, she ventured onto the wooden dance floor, making sure to stay out of the direct line of fire of the bouquet. No way did she want to be a target. If it weren't for the fact she was sure Gadiya would have marched over and dragged her onto the floor, she would have never subjected herself to this ridiculous tradition.

Gadiya turned her back and teased the group of women a few times with a false release. The room burst into laughter as several women reacted prematurely and came inches from busting their asses. When Gadiya finally released the fresh flowers, it soared past the sea of grabbing hands and landed right in Rana's arms as if they'd been a beacon for the mound of pink and white roses.

Rana gasped in disbelief and eyed the plush arrangement she'd helped Gadiya pick out. The room cheered her fortune. A handful of the woman who'd vied for the bundle either scowled or rolled their eyes. Since she wasn't above a little pettiness every now and then, she waved her bounty through the air as if she'd actually appreciated catching it.

A short time later, the single women cleared the floor to make room for the eligible bachelors. An impressive collection of men gathered, but none as riveting as Dallas. When Nico released the garter, the men parted like the Red Sea. Either Dallas had been preoccupied or not fast enough, because he didn't budge. The narrow band of fabric cut through the air like a missile, exploding into his chest.

If Rana hadn't known any better, she would have sworn Gadiya had somehow arranged this. Men clapped Dallas on the shoulders and back, revealing their relief that it wasn't them who'd caught the blue and white trinket. The planner summoned Rana to join Dallas for pictures. Now, more than ever, Rana regretted catching the bouquet.

A glance at Gadiya reinforced her belief that somehow, someway the woman had orchestrated this. It could have been the somehow-someway-I-orchestrated-this guilty expression on her face. Rana flashed her own declaration in return. One that stated: You will pay for this.

"Closer," the planner instructed, practically forcing Rana against Dallas.

Rana had intentionally maintained a safe distance. From across the room, he'd had an effect on her body. Standing too close to him would surely short-circuit her system. The energy radiating from him had already scrambled her brain. And his scent—manly and delicious—had butterflies performing circus tricks in her stomach.

The photographer needed to move things along before she collapsed from desire. There were so many snap, snap, snaps and flash, flash, flashes, Rana lost count. After posing for what felt like a million and one pictures with Dallas, she attempted to make a smooth getaway.

"You're not going to escape before you dance with me, are you?" Dallas asked.

His smooth, sexy tone feathered her skin like gentle bedroom kisses. Not wanting to reveal how being so close to him affected her, Rana did her best at playing it cool. Despite feeling as if her flesh was about to melt off the bone because of the intense heat their chemistry generated.

"I..." She searched frantically for a plausible excuse. Nothing came. Why in the hell did this man have her so shaken? Probably because she hadn't been this attracted to a man in a long time.

Admittedly, she'd been far more confident flirting with him from across the room. Standing close to him had her so rattled she could hardly think straight—or crooked, for that matter. *Get it together, girl. You can handle three minutes with the man. You got this*. Flashing a nervous smile, she said, "Sure."

A beat later, L.T.D's "Love Ballad" poured

through the speakers. A hint of concern rushed through Rana. This song was *at least* eight minutes long. Three she could do. But eight?

"Something wrong?" Dallas asked.

If you excluded the fact she wanted to take off across the room... "Um, no."

The burn of desire seared her the second Dallas's strong arms closed around her, hugging her to his solid frame. He felt good. So damn good. Too damn good. As a means of self-preservation, she put a sliver of distance between them.

Much good it did. His energy was just too powerful. It summoned her body close to his again. Or it could have been the hand Dallas placed on the small of her back right before pulling her back to him. Rana closed her eyes and moaned, then prayed the sound of seduction had only been in her head.

Weren't they simply supposed to snap a few pictures together, then go their separate ways? Yet, here she stood in his arms, trying her best not to buckle under the pressure. Why was she torturing herself like this?

Maybe because there was something about Dallas Fontaine that stimulated her curiosity, and her body.

***

Regardless of where Dallas had moved about the room throughout the night, he found himself seeking out Rana. He'd never been so damn attracted to a woman in his life. Now here he was pressed against her body so tight that she felt like a delicate second skin.

And to think, he'd almost brushed off the opportunity to catch the garter. But once she'd caught the bouquet, the decision had been made.

He was beyond happy he'd opted to join the rest of the eligible bachelors on the floor. He bet if the other men had known they'd get the chance to slow-dance with Rana, they wouldn't have been so quick to avoid catching the piece.

He'd watched men drool over her all night, a scene that had bothered him far more than it should have, given the fact that she wasn't his. *Yet,* he told himself. Their chemistry was too potent not to explore.

His eyes glided over one of her bare, brown shoulders. The gorgeous woman had played in his thoughts—and fantasies—since he'd been introduced to his good friend and boss's then future sister-in-law.

Breathtaking had been the first term to pop in his head when his eyes had raked over Rana's soft brown skin and perfect curves. One look into her gentle brown eyes and he'd been a goner. From what he'd learned about Rana, she wouldn't be easily wooed. Which meant he had to bring his A-game. Good thing he never left home without it.

He'd harbored major regret when he'd first arrived from D.C. to join the Mount Pleasance Fire

Department, but small-town living wasn't looking too cumbersome after all.

"I love this song," he said, breaking the silence between them.

"Yeah, it feels so amazing—"

Her body tensed in his arms. The slip-up brought a smile to his face. Yeah, she was feeling him, too. Though he'd expected that from the way they'd eye-flirted earlier. The thoughts that had filled his head as he'd stared across at her were severe enough to have him banned from some countries.

Tilting her head to eye him, she said, "*Sounds* amazing, I meant to say."

His eyes trailed from hers and settled on her lips, brushed with the sexiest shade of pink he'd ever seen on any woman. The desire to crush his mouth to hers and kiss her until she begged for far more than his mouth rippled through him like a massive quake.

A stir in his crotch forced him to think of something less taxing than how delicious he was sure she'd taste. Connecting with her gaze again, he said, "So, what are you going to do with the flowers?"

Rana's eyes slid to the bouquet partially resting on his shoulder. "Toss it as soon as I get a chance."

He arched a curious brow. "Do you have something against marriage?"

"Not at all. I'm just not a big fan of flowers."

"Huh." That was a first. The women he encountered loved flowers. And expected them often. Yeah, he'd been right. Rana Lassiter was different. "Well, that's good to know."

She eyed him quizzically, but before she could ask the swirling question he saw in her eyes, they were rudely interrupted.

"Mind if I cut in?"

Dallas glanced down at the intrusion. A brown-skinned man wearing a crisp white shirt and gray slacks. Dallas's jaw tightened at the confident expression on the man's face. *Hell no!* danced on the tip of his tongue, but he swallowed the salty words. For now, he'd play nice.

Dallas reluctantly released Rana, thanked her for the dance and made his way across the room to the open-bar. "Whiskey neat."

"You sure you can handle such a manly drink?" came from behind.

Dallas turned to see Nico Dupree—fire chief, his new boss and one of his best friends. "Make that two," Dallas told the bartender.

Nico held up his hand. "Oh, no. Last time I drank hard liquor with this brother, I was nearly arrested."

Both men rolled with laughter.

"Good times," Dallas said.

"Indeed," said Nico.

"Marriage looks good on you, man. Got you glowing and shit," Dallas said, taking a sip from his glass. "I'm glad things finally worked out for one of us."

Dallas thought back to his previous life in D.C., then allowed the short memories to fade.

"Man..." Nico stared across at his wife. "I count my blessings every single day. I love that woman in a way I can't even begin to put into words."

Dallas hoped to one day be able to say the same about someone. He fought seeking out Rana. What was it about that woman that drew him in? Refocusing on Nico, who was still admiring his new bride, Dallas said, "You're not about to cry are you?" Dallas flashed a palm. "Don't get me wrong, it's nothing wrong with a grown man crying. I just need to prepare myself."

Nico barked a laughed. "Kiss my ass. No, I'm not about to cry."

"Just checking. You were looking a little misty-eyed."

"Was it the same misty-eyed look you had when you let Todd jack Rana from you."

Dallas's gaze instantly slid toward the dance floor. *Todd.* So that was the bastard's name, huh? "Is that her man?"

"Todd? Ha! He wishes."

That was promising. Dallas took a nonchalant sip from his glass as his eyes roamed over Rana's toned frame. Something all of the Lassiter sisters had in common was those dangerous curves. However, Rana's was outrageous. Like an hourglass with extra glass at the hips. If he had his way, he'd pull her into a back room inside the reception hall, strip her out of that dress and bend her over a desk—chair—anything, everything, and bury himself so deep inside of her he'd need GPS to get out.

Damn, he'd love to tangle his fingers through her soft curls, while planting tender kisses all over her body. Especially her neck. Yeah, that neck was meant for his lips and his lips only. *Not Todd's*. His teeth clenched and he growled to himself at the mention of the man's name.

Nico dabbed a napkin against Dallas's face. "Is that a tear I see glistening in the corner of your eye?"

Hell, it might very well have been a tear. The idea of making sweet love to Rana stirred all kinds of emotions. "Would you have an issue with me asking Rana out?"

"Not at all. You're a good brother. She needs a good brother in her life."

He knew a little something about being a good dude, even if he hadn't always practiced being one. *A changed man*, he reminded himself.

"But I will warn you...once a Lassiter woman gets into your system, there's no getting her out. Trust me, I know."

Dallas knew Nico's history with Gadiya—how he'd loved her and lost her. Dallas was glad they'd found their way back to one another. Simply being in the room with the two of them for any length of time, you just knew they were meant to be.

Meant to be. He laughed to himself. He'd only been in Mount Pleasance two weeks, and the place was already buffing away his rough exterior. But if true love really did exist, those two personified it.

Nico clapped Dallas on the shoulder. "And speaking of Lassiter women, I have to get back to mine."

They shared a manly hug before Nico made his way back to his bride.

When Dallas sought Rana on the dance floor, she was nowhere in sight. Damn, he'd only turned away for a moment. How could she have escaped? Todd had vanished, too. Had they left together? Maybe Nico had been wrong. Maybe Rana and Todd were an item. A knot formed in the pit of his stomach, then tightened when he thought about Todd doing intimate things with Rana.

The strands loosened when he spotted Rana chatting with a group of women. Though all were attractive, they couldn't hold a candle stick to Rana. Maybe one. Rana's sisters Sadona. Only because they looked so much alike. Still, Rana was the one who did it big time for him.

Downing the rest of his drink, he made his way across the room to finish what they'd started earlier. All eyes fixed on him as he neared. The very pregnant woman who'd been talking clammed up, which led him to believe he'd been the topic of discussion. A good or bad thing, depending on what was being said. But how bad could the chatter have been? Other than Nico, no one knew him or the Fontaine name in Mount Pleasance, which made it the perfect place to start anew.

With her back to him, Rana was the last to realize his approach. She jolted when she turned. Either he'd startled her or she was completely stunned by his devastatingly good looks. He claimed the latter.

"Dallas?" she said.

Her gorgeous mouth curled into a hesitant smile as if she wasn't sure to be happy or dismayed by his presence. Either way, he wasn't going anywhere. "Hey." He slid his gaze from Rana's. "Ladies."

Rana made the introductions. The very pregnant woman, Davena, stuck out her hand.

"Nice to meet you. You're replacing my fiancé, Ollie. Thank you."

Dallas captured the appreciative woman's hand. Nico had mentioned the near-fatal fire that had occurred a few months back and how he and Ollie had barely escaped with their lives. From what he'd been told, Davena had all but demanded Ollie quit the department. Understandable. "You're welcome. I think."

Laughter sounded, followed by the ladies excusing themselves one-by-one. Dallas hadn't missed the look Rana's sister flashed her as she moved away. Now, what was that all about? Girl code was sometimes hard to decipher. He chuckled. *Women*.

Rana eyed him. "What's so funny?"

The primal way I want to rip you out of that damn dress. Of course, he kept that to himself. "Nothing." He started to ask her to dance again, but there were two things he couldn't risk: being interrupted again and the torture of having her body so close to him and not being able to use his hands to explore every inch of it.

A beat of silence played between them, which was okay because he was more than content staring into her mesmerizing eyes.

"So, how are you liking Mount Pleasance?" Rana asked.

"Things are looking very promising."

"Really?"

Her gaze left him and traveled to his mouth. He had the feeling she was having a few naughty thoughts of her own. When she flinched, as if realizing what she was doing, he was sure of it.

"So, is Todd my competition?"

Rana laughed, then sobered, folding her arms across her chest. "Your competition? Sounds like you're wanting to get to know me better, Mr. Fontaine."

Dallas slid his hands into his pockets. "Is that a problem, Ms. Lassiter?"

Rana was quiet for a moment. "Your boss is my brother-in-law."

"Is that a problem?" he echoed again.

She studied him. "Normally, no. But unfortunately—"

"Good," he said, cutting off her objection.

Instead of saying more, he winked and strolled away. Most women liked a little intrigue. He was gambling on Rana being among the masses.

2

Instead of being in her warm bed at four in the morning, Rana stood naked—because painting nude gave her inspiration—inside her converted guest bedroom now serving as her in-home paint studio, firing away at the canvas. This image had been burned into her thoughts the second she'd experienced Dallas up close and personal, blaring as brightly as a neon sign operating in pitch black. She'd tried ignoring it since she'd returned home from Gadiya and Nico's wedding reception two hours ago, but she couldn't.

Four hours later, she scrutinized her creation. Tilting her head to the left, then to the right, she was both exhausted and turned on in all the same breath. "Just need one last—" She paused mid-stroke when she thought she heard the doorbell ring. Lowering her neo-soul, she listened.

Ding.

Her brows knitted and gaze slid to the wall clock. Who was visiting her at eight o'clock in the morning? And on a Sunday. And without calling first. Apparently, whomever it was didn't know her on a personal level. If so, they'd have known better. Sundays were usually her sleep-in days.

She refocused on the painting. Dallas was already complicating her life, and she wasn't even dating or sleeping with him. One she really wanted to do, the other—

The doorbell dinged again. *Ugh*. She hated to be interrupted in the middle of creating. Maybe if she ignored whoever it was, they'd go away. She studied the once white canvas, now covered with two intimately tangled bodies sharing a sensual dance, making love... It all depended on the angle in which you observed the painting.

Ding.

"Dammit."

Obviously, her pest wasn't getting the hint. Shrugging into a robe, she stalked out of the bedroom and to the front door, yanking it open. A strong back, broad shoulders, tight ass, and muscular thighs greeted her. Clearing her throat, Dallas stopped mid-descent, turned and moved toward her.

The sight of him was better than any cup of coffee she could have consumed. Like caffeine, he gave her a jolt of energy.

"Good morning," he said.

Rana folded her arms across her chest and leaned against the door frame. "Good morning."

"I know I should have called first but realized at the last minute I didn't have your phone number."

"Ah. Well, perhaps you could have gotten it from the same place you got my address."

Dallas lowered his head, chuckled, and smoothed a large hand down the side of his stubbled cheek. While he processed being called out, her eyes dropped to the dark gray T-shirt he wore. *Mmm, mmm, mmm*. His body gave her all types of sinful inspiration.

Allowing her eyes to crawl back up his frame, she said, "What are you doing here? And let's try the truth this time."

"I really wanted to see you," he said plainly.

His expression was so stern it startled her. Flashing a semblance of strength, she said, "Now, that wasn't so hard, right?"

"For me...yeah, it kinda was."

"What, do you have a problem with the truth?"

Dallas flashed a half-smile. "Nope. I have a great appreciation for the truth."

"Uh-huh. So, Dallas Fontaine, tell me again what you're doing on my porch? At eight o'clock. On a Sunday morning."

"I was hoping you'd allow me to take you to breakfast."

When he lifted a bag from her favorite bakery, her suspicion rose. There was only one way he could have known she loved The Buttered Croissant. *Gadiya*.

Dallas continued, "Then afterward, maybe a stroll around the square. Sit on a bench. Chat. Get to know each other. What do you say?"

"This sounds an awful lot like a date to me."

"We can call it whatever you like." He made a motion to enter, but Rana blocked him by propping her leg against the doorjamb.

The silky burgundy fabric parted, revealing her entire left leg and the lion paws tattoo trailing up her thigh. Dallas's eyes lowered to her exposed flesh. A sound she was sure she wasn't supposed to hear rumbled in his chest.

"Or we could just hang out here on the porch for a while. The view is fantastic."

A second later, Rana's leg fell, and Dallas brushed past her. The scent of his cologne was like an aphrodisiac and sent blood rushing to all of her sensitive parts. Ignoring the ache between her legs and the tightening of her nipples, she closed her eyes for a brief moment. *What in the hell was she getting herself into*?

***

Dallas scrutinized the inside of the bungalow style home. The décor was simple, yet suited the quaint residence and its owner, though his mother would have thought differently about the furnishings. The woman would have given the house a complete overhaul, fashioning it with the most expensive and elegant pieces she could find. One thing his mother was good at, spending money.

His eyes slid to several unpacked cardboard boxes scattered around. "Did you just move in?"

"A few months ago," she said, biting at the corner of her lip.

"Oh." He shrugged. "Yeah, these things take

time. Gotta find the perfect placement for everything." He fought the urge to volunteer to unpack and break down the boxes. Clutter was not his thing. Plus, it presented a fire hazard. "Did I wake you?"

"No. I was painting."

"Painting? You paint?"

"Don't sound so surprised."

"It's not that. I just..." He allowed his words to trail before he put his foot in his mouth. "May I see some of your work."

"I'm not sure you're ready for my bedroom brushings."

"Bedroom brushings? Now I have to see them."

Rana studied him for a moment. "Down the hall second door on the right. I'll join you in a sec."

He nodded, then followed her directions. The second he walked into the room, he was transported into a world of sensual seduction that welcomed him like an old family friend. His eyes fixed on the painting of a female form stretched out on a cream-colored chaise lounge chair, her hair flowing over one shoulder. A throw in the same color as the chair partially covered her breasts, leaving just enough to the imagination. The face was hidden by a wide brim hat.

The piece hung on a wall all by itself, nothing else there to distract from the...the... absolutely mind-blowing piece.

Seconds later, he heard a squeal, then bare

feet padding down the hall. “Dallas, wait! Don’t—” If Rana was attempting to keep him from seeing this masterpiece, too late.

Not pulling his eyes away from the entrancing work, he said, “I want this one.” Just like Rana, something about it appealed to him.

She stood beside him. “It’s not for sale.”

“Everything has a price.”

“I’m not for sale.”

Dallas whipped his head toward her. “That’s…you?”

She nodded.

That wholly explained his draw to the piece. “How much?”

“You like getting your way, don’t you?”

“Who doesn’t?”

“And something tells me you usually get it.”

He shrugged one shoulder. “I do.” It sounded conceited, but it was the truth.

“Well, I would hate to be the one who wrecked your flawless track record. If you want me—*it*,” she corrected—“twenty thousand, and it’s yours.”

A wicked smile curled her beautiful lips. It was all he could do to keep from smashing his mouth to hers. “Ouch.”

She laughed. “I think one of these might work better for your pockets.”

Rana led him to a photo gallery of images affixed to another wall, a four-digit number printed on the bottom right corner. An order number, he assumed.

"You can find all of these on my website. We should—"

Then he saw it. A magnificent display. Not against the wall but on a wooden easel a few feet away. How in the hell had he missed it? This...this beautifully seductive tangling of bodies, still wet with fresh paint. This must have been the piece Rana had been working on when he arrived. Was this why she'd been so eager to rescind his invitation into the room?

"*Wow*. This is..." Arousing as hell, he wanted to say, but said instead, "amazing." He eyed her. "You are truly talented, you know that?"

A smile twitched at her lips. "Thank you. It's my therapy."

"Will this be available on your website?"

She hesitated to answer for a moment, her eyes settling on her latest creation. "Yes. Well...maybe. I don't know about this one just yet."

Dallas slid his attention back to the print. The two lovers on the surface could easily have been the two of them. Embracing, kissing, making hot passionate love. Blood rushed to his crotch, and he felt himself swell. *Shit*. He filled his thoughts with an image of a baseball field, a hundred and ten-year-old lady on the pitchers' mound.

"Dallas?"

"We should eat," he said, leading the way out of the room before he allowed his fantasies of taking Rana right there on the hardwood floor to get him in trouble.

While Rana went to change, he set up the assortment of bagels, cream cheese, fruit, and muffins he'd gotten from the bakery in town. When he'd driven Nico and Gadiya to the airport that morning, Gadiya had nonchalantly mentioned Rana loved this place. She'd also innocently mentioned Rana being single and had inquired about his status. "Single," he had said, bringing a wide smile to the scheming woman's face.

"Impressive," Rana said, entering behind him.

He turned. "I—" The words froze in his throat. Rana glided toward him like a sexy lioness. The fitted pink tank top accented her impressive breasts. Denim shorts that looked as if they'd once been jeans gave him a second glance at the shapely thigh he'd gotten a glimpse of earlier. Again, his thoughts went haywire.

Barefooted, she stood directly in front of him. In heels, they'd almost been able to see eye to eye. Now, she needed to tip her head to look into his eyes. With one swift motion, he could have her in his arms. *Not yet,* he told himself. His gaze trailed to her mouth. *But soon.*

"I may be putting my foot in my mouth when I say this, but you look tired," he said.

"Wow. Talk about a blow to a girl's self-esteem."

"Something tells me it'll take a lot more than that to bruise you."

"You're right. And yes, I am tired. New-puppy-play-hard-and-drop, tired. I was up all night painting. When inspiration strikes…"

"Inspiration, huh?" Her words led him to his next question. "Did something," *or someone*, "at the reception act as your muse?"

She eyed him with an expression that suggested she knew what he was hinting at.

"There's inspiration all around," she said, smirking, then strolling toward the sofa and dropping down.

He joined her. In a bold move, he captured her hand and intertwined his fingers with hers. The fact she didn't snatch away was a good sign, right? "I like you, Rana Lassiter."

Her eyes slid to their joined hands, then met his gaze. "You don't even know me, Dallas Fontaine."

"But I want to." He gave her a severe look just so she'd know how serious he was about getting to know her.

She stared at him for a long moment, not uttering a word. Nico had told him how Gadiya had sprinted away from him when he'd proposed to her. He hoped running from dicey situations wasn't a Lassiter gene Rana had inherited.

Nah, she wasn't a runner. Rana struck him as someone who faced things head-on.

"Are you always so direct?" she finally said.

"No. I hold back when necessary. I just don't often find it necessary."

"I'm not looking for a relationship right now,

Dallas. Been there done that."

"What are you looking for?" She didn't need to answer for him to know exactly what she wanted. Sex with no strings. There was a time in the not-so-distant past when he would have jumped all over her unspoken proposition. Not this time. "Ah," was all he said. He kissed the back of her hand, released it and stood. "I'll clean up, then let you get some rest."

Rana came to her feet. "Wait, you're...leaving?"

The expression on her face suggested she couldn't believe he would pass up an opportunity to sleep with her. To be honest, neither could he. Maybe it was the fact that he'd never been this attracted to any woman. Maybe it was watching Nico and Gadiya pledge their love to one another. Maybe it was his recently turning thirty-six. Hell, he didn't know. All he knew was he wanted more than just sex with Rana. "Meaningless sex really isn't my thing," he said.

Her beautiful lips parted, but nothing came out. Clearly, she was at a loss for words. Shock, then embarrassment, then sadness played on her gorgeous face. It stripped a layer of his confidence away.

"Rana—"

"I'll clean this up. Thank you for stopping by with breakfast. I'm sure it is delicious."

She shifted away from him and started doing busy work on the table. Her cold shoulder gave him chills. Instead of arguing with her, he said, "Okay." He made a motion to leave, but paused. "You should consider the fact that maybe you went there and done that with the wrong one. I don't want just your body, Rana. I want you." When she slowly faced him, he leaned forward and placed a kiss on her cheek. "Get some rest, beautiful."

A huge smile curled his lips as he moved to his SUV. Rana didn't know it yet, but she would be his. Or maybe she did. In which case, he'd give her a little time to get comfortable with the notion.

3

For the past few weeks, all Rana had thought about was Dallas. Even now, standing in Gadiya's kitchen with her sisters, preparing Sunday dinner, his handsome face danced in her head like tempting sugarplums. *Get the hell out of my head, Dallas Fontaine*. She hacked at a potato in frustration.

In an attempt to fade him from her thoughts, she hadn't shared with either of her sisters what had transpired between her and Dallas at her place, which was difficult because she told her sisters everything. But if she shared the details with them, they both would urge her to give Dallas a chance. She wasn't sure she was ready to travel down this road again.

She replayed her last encounter with Dallas and cringed. Had she actually offered him *meaningless sex,* as he'd put it? He'd been wrong. It would have meant something. It would have meant she'd finally gotten what she'd been needing. But wasn't that selfish, to only consider her own needs? *Maybe.*

Heck, it didn't matter anyway. He'd turned her down. She paused. Had he actually shot her down? *I don't just want your body. I want you*. The words had stayed with her and made her all warm and fuzzy inside every time she recalled them. But warm and fuzzy usually got her in trouble.

Ugh. Why had she allowed this man to get into her head like this? A man she barely knew.

"What!"

The alarm in Gadiya's voice startled Rana back to reality. Quickly counting her fingers, she whipped her head toward Gadiya and Sadona. "What's wrong?"

"Did you not just hear your sister?" Gadiya said. "She and Alec are getting a divorce."

Rana's mouth fell open. Sadona had given her bits and pieces over the past couple of weeks but had kept this vital detail to herself. Apparently, she'd wanted to wait until they were all together to drop this major bomb. "Divorced?" She knew they were having problems, but—divorced. "What—"

"He had an affair," Sadona said plainly. "I can't forgive that type of betrayal. I—" Her voice cracked, and she swallowed hard. Starting again, she said, "I tried, but I can't. We're separated. Have been for six months."

"*Six months!*" Gadiya said.

Sadona nodded. When tears glistened in her eyes, both Rana and Gadiya wrapped their arms around her for comfort and support.

"Oh, sweetie, I'm so sorry," Rana said.

"Me, too," Gadiya added.

"Neither one of you are to blame." She squeezed them tightly. "But thank you."

The doorbell rang, and Nico called out from somewhere in the house, "I got it."

"Are you sure you're okay, sis?" Gadiya asked.

Sadona flashed a low-wattage smile. "Yes. I've made peace with it."

Rana stroked Sadona's arms. "Why didn't you tell us what you were going through? You know we would have been there for you."

"I just needed to process it all on my own. I'm okay, really. I've done all the crying I'm going to do over him."

Rana certainly knew what it was like to love and lose someone. Her heart ached for Sadona because she knew all too well how this type of pain could cripple you.

"One good thing will come out of this," Sadona continued. "I'm coming home."

Both Rana's and Gadiya's eyes widened simultaneously. "You're moving back to Mount Pleasance?" They asked in unison.

When Sadona nodded, they both squealed like schoolgirls. They'd both wished on numerous occasions that Sadona would move back home. Though Rana was thrilled their wish had come true, she hated it was under these circumstances.

Nico raced into the kitchen, his eyes sweeping the room. "What's wrong?"

Rana parted her lips to speak, but the sight of Dallas strolling in behind Nico froze the words on the tip of her tongue. What was he doing here, dressed so impeccably in a pair of gray slacks and red pullover shirt? The answer came to her fairly quickly.

Gadiya strikes again, she thought, unable to

pull her attention away from Dallas long enough to scowl at her gung-ho sibling. Lord, this man wore fabric well. How much more of him could her system take without overloading and shutting down.

Then he winked at her.

Typically, such a benign action would not have triggered a reaction out of Rana, but Dallas's winks were like arousing kisses to the most intimate parts of her body. The innocent gesture caused a not-so-innocent effect on her.

Innocent gesture? Maybe she should reconsider that claim.

"Everything's all right, sweetheart," Gadiya assured Nico.

Snatching her eyes away from Dallas, Rana added, "Yeah. We just got the best news ever. Sadona is moving back home."

"That's great news," Nico said, moving toward Sadona. "Welcome home, sis." He gave her a brotherly hug. "You have just made these women extremely happy."

"Dallas," Gadiya said.

She appeared surprised by his presence, though Rana highly doubted that was the case. But the stunned expression had been a nice touch. Considering there was a possibility Dallas could have been invited by Nico, Rana held off assigning blame.

Gadiya continued, "Welcome. I'm glad you decided to join this crazy bunch for dinner."

"I wouldn't have missed it for the world."

When Dallas tossed a brief glance in Rana's direction, the air in the room grew thick.

"Rana, you remember Dallas, right?"

Yes, but she wished she could forget him. "I do. Nice seeing you again, Dallas." The polite thing to do would have been to offer her hand, but she wasn't prepared to risk the impact of his touch.

"Likewise."

His gaze lingered on her for several uncomfortable seconds. Whatever he was searching for, she hoped he found it soon. The temperature in the room felt as if it rose several degrees, and her heart rate kicked up a notch. It wasn't until Dallas finally looked away that she realize she'd been holding her breath. Releasing it in a slow, steady stream, she vowed that Dallas would not get the best of her.

Dallas passed Gadiya the bottle of wine he'd entered with. "This is for you. Thanks again for the invite."

Ah-ha. Confirmation. This had been Gadiya's doing. Rana had allowed her sister's deceptive practices at the reception to go unchecked; she wouldn't get off so easily this time. When Nico and Dallas excused themselves from the room, Rana slid a narrow-eyed gaze at Gadiya.

Gadiya shrugged. "What?"

Rana jabbed a finger at her. In a muted tone, she said, "You're not slick. I know what you're doing."

Gadiya flashed an utterly insulted expression and rested her hands on her hips. “I have absolutely no idea what you’re talking about, Rana Lassiter. I am not trying to set you up with that good-looking specimen, Dallas Fontaine. Nope, I sure am not.”

“*Shh*,” Rana hissed, tossing a glance at the door Dallas and Nico had walked through moments earlier.

Sadona laughed. “Yeah, she’s up to no good. But you do have to admit, Ra, you two would make a gorgeous couple. Plus, he’s totally into you.”

“Totally,” Gadiya co-signed.

“Oh my God. Not you too. Is this what I have to look forward to? You two ganging up on me?”

“*Yes!*” Gadiya and Sadona said in unison.

They shared a laugh.

Gadiya smirked. “We’ve established that Dallas is totally into you. Now the question is…are you totally into him?”

Gadiya and Sadona eyed her as if she gave the correct answer they’d each win a million dollars. Smirking, Rana returned to peeling the potato she’d abandoned, leaving them in suspense. Truth was, Dallas Fontaine had certainly piqued her curiosity. And maybe, just maybe, she was a little into him, too. Unfortunately, he wanted more than she was prepared to offer.

***

Several additional guests had arrived for Sunday dinner at the Dupree House. A few Dallas knew, others he didn't. A middle-aged man who called himself Greenville—"nothing else, just Greenville," he'd stated—sat beside him. Dallas got the impression something was a little wrong with the man, mainly because for the past ten minutes he'd been rearranging his silverware.

But it was the individual seated directly across from him at the twelve-person table that had garnered most of his attention for the past hour. *Rana*. Something told him her placement hadn't been coincidental. Gadiya wasn't very subtle in her attempt to pair them up.

While people chatted around him, his eyes raked over Rana. Her big doe eyes, perfect mouth, chin, neck, ample breasts—pressed nicely against the navy blue blouse she wore. Feeling the tightening in the pit of his stomach should have signaled him to look away, but he was powerless against this woman. It amused and angered him.

"How are you liking Mount Pleasance, Dallas?"

Gadiya's words caused Rana to glance in his direction, something she'd avoided until now.

"Dallas, Texas. Dallas Cowboys. Dallas Mavericks," Greenville said, not bothering to halt his task. "Cool name. Dallas. Cool name. Not better than Greenville, though."

The laughter at the table didn't seem to faze Greenville; he just kept right on arranging.

Sobering, Dallas pinned his eyes to Rana's. "I

was a little skeptical at first. But after exploring the town and getting to know folks, I think I'm going to love it here."

A visually rattled Rana lifted her glass to her lips. Man, he envied drink-ware.

"You should get Rana to show you around town. She's a natural GPS," Gadiya said.

Rana choked on the sweet tea and coughed ferociously. "Excuse me," she said, pushing away from the table and escaping the room.

Gadiya scooted out her chair, but Dallas was out of his before she could get to her feet. "I'll check on her."

Gadiya beamed a high-wattage smile, then eyed Sadona and smirked. "Okay."

When Dallas entered the kitchen, Rana had her eyes closed and a hand resting on her forehead. This would have been the perfect time for a blitz attack, rushing to her and kissing her senseless. He resisted the urge. "Was the suggestion that bad?"

Her eyes popped open. Her startled gaze slid past him as if expecting to see someone standing behind him. She folded her arms over her chest, then lowered them to her sides. Was he making her nervous?

"Dallas?"

By the confused look on her face, he concluded she'd been expecting one of her sisters. Anyone but him.

"Um...no. It wasn't..." She rested a hand on

her collarbone. “Did you need something?”

Now that was a dangerous question. He would need wallpaper to list all of the things he needed. To hold her, to kiss her, to make love to her. The list could go on and on for days. “No. Just wanted to check on you.”

A faint smile twitched at the corner of her mouth, one he was fairly sure she was attempting to hide.

“That was mighty thoughtful of you. But as you can see, I’m fine. We should probably get back before Gadiya sends out a search party.”

Rana released a nervous laugh, then attempted to brush past him. Dallas hooked an arm around her waist, thwarting her escape. She gasped, rested her warm hands on his forearm and turned her head toward him. With her eyes latched to his, an intense, silent, lust-filled moment played between them. Reeling her in, they stood toe-to-toe.

Rana pressed her hands into his chest but didn’t push away. “Dallas—”

Before she could mount a protest, before he could come to his good sense, he kissed her. His fate was sealed the second his lips touched hers. He kissed her hard, raw, passionately, possessively. He took, and he gave. Greed filled him, fighting for supremacy over his desire. Something took over his body, causing him to try his best to consume Rana.

The room felt as if it were quaking, but he didn’t stop ravishing her mouth. Couldn’t stop...even if he'd wanted to. He clung to her like a wet leaf on a gutter. Her mouth—hot, wet, delicious—easily became his weakness. Raging heat burned through him, pooling its fury in his crotch.

He swelled.

He ached.

He desperately needed.

Rana moaned as his hands explored her backside, moved along the dip of her back, crawled up her sides and came to rest on either side of her neck. He backed her against the sub-zero refrigerator, deepening their dangerous connection.

Everything about the kiss was perfect. The way her tongue greedily sparred with his. The way heat from her mouth rushed into his. The way their lips fitted seamlessly together. Perfect. All of it.

But it wasn't enough.

His hunger—selfish desire—for her was unlike anything he'd ever known, ever experienced. If he'd been granted one wish, it would have been for this moment to never end.

A second later, he realized he'd jinxed himself with the thought. Mild resistance from Rana's delicate hands pressed into his heaving chest. *No*, he said to himself, not wanting her to end this magnificent moment.

"We're going to get caught, Dallas," she said against their joined mouths.

"I don't give a damn about the risks." All he

wanted was to continue experiencing this intense pleasure. His painful erection pressed against his zipper. Guiding his pelvis forward, he pressed his hardness into her stomach.

As if the feel of him startled her, she snatched away. Apart, their chests rose and fell in tandem. Their eyes locked in a battle of wills, neither daring to turn away. They wanted—needed—the same thing.

Dallas closed the gap between them. “I want you.”

Never faltering, she said, “You had a chance to have me.”

He shook his head. “Like I told you before, I don’t just want your body, Rana. I want you.”

Rana’s lips parted, but before she could say whatever was on her mind, Greenville sauntered into the room. A string of swears bounced around in Dallas’s head. Talk about bad freaking timing.

“Dallas, Texas. Dallas Cowboys. Dallas Mavericks. Cool name.”

Rana put some distance between her and Dallas. “Do you need something, Greenville?”

“Bathroom, painting lady.”

“It’s down the hall, remember?”

“Yeah. Yeah. Down the hall.” He turned and was gone, mumbling something under his breath.

Dallas wanted to pick up where they’d left off, but the look in Rana’s eyes told him he wouldn’t get another opportunity to taste her sweet mouth. At least, not tonight. *It was good while it lasted.*

"We really should get back," she said, dashing toward the door.

"I have something for you." His words stopped Rana dead in her tracks. When she turned, her brows were knotted tightly.

"Something for me?"

Reaching into his pocket, he retrieved an envelope and passed it to her.

"What is this?" Tearing into the enclosure, she gasped. "What...Why?" Her eyes darted toward him.

Dallas rested a hand behind her neck, positioning his mouth inches from hers. "Please make sure my paintings aren't damaged during delivery."

Rana's bottom lip trembled, and the temptation to kiss her nearly buckled his knees. *Resist, man*. Forcing his feet to move, he stepped past her and left the room.

4

For the past three days, Rana had only been able to think about two things: the electrifying kiss Dallas had planted on her inside Gadiya and Nico's kitchen, and the twenty-five thousand dollar check he'd placed in her hands. *Twenty-five thousand dollars.* Where in the hell had Dallas gotten money like this?

Lifting the cashier's check from her desk, she eyed it for the umpteenth time. He wanted two things—well, three if you counted her. And damn if she didn't want him, too. Far more than she was willing to admit to anyone but her inner self.

Twenty thousand dollars for a painting of me. And another five thousand for the painting of us. Us? She shook her head but didn't correct herself because it was the two of them. Making love to Dallas was exactly what she'd had in mind when she'd created the piece.

Where in the hell had he gotten twenty-five thousand dollars? Had he dipped into his 401K? Taken out a loan? Considering those options, she felt awful for not immediately returning the check. How much could the Mount Pleasance Fire Department actually pay? It wasn't like they were in New York or Chicago. He'd have to work a helluva lot of overtime to recoup this kind of money.

The idea of him going to such a ridiculous extent to get her attention curled her lips. And she had to admit, it felt good to be chased, instead of being the one doing the chasing. A frown replaced the smile when she thought about her ex, Walton.

They'd dated a little over two years. Then, out of the blue, he'd ended things by saying they wanted different things. All she'd wanted was him. Shamefully, she'd spent months chasing him like a dog in heat. Chasing after a man who didn't want her. Had she really been so stupid? And desperate?

Luckily, she'd come to her senses. And when she'd stopped pursuing him, he'd wanted her. Wasn't that how it always went? Thankfully, by that point, she'd discovered she was better off without him. Plus, she'd unearthed the real reason he'd ended their relationship so abruptly. A woman who turned out to be a gold-digger and had stolen every dime of his savings.

As much as she hated to admit it, the whole ordeal with Walton had done a number on her self-esteem. Lassiter women weren't weak woman, but she'd certainly had a weak moment. One that, if she were truly being honest, was playing a part in her resistance of Dallas.

Pushing back in her chair, she released a heavy sigh and closed her eyes. In the stillness, her mother's words rang in her ears. *Your past can shape your future. For good or for bad.*

Two taps at her office door forced Rana's eyes open. Tyrell, her stock-boy slash cashier slash delivery guy slash maintenance man slash security guard, peeped his head into the room. Last week, his headful of unruly curls had been purple. Today, they were blue with a blonde streak smack-dab in the center. If nothing else, he was creative. The perfect fit for her arts and crafts store.

"Doll, you have a vi...si...tor."

By the way he closed his eyes and moan, it was a good-looking man. And with a reaction like this, there was only one guess as to whom it was. "Send him back."

"Okay."

Rana lunged forward in her chair. "No! Wait. On second thought, I'll come up." She couldn't risk Dallas laying another one of those kisses on her. Moaning coming from her office would not have been a good look.

Standing, she ironed a hand down the front of her red polo shirt. Why in the hell was she so nervous? She didn't do nervous. She did composed and firm. *Composed and firm*, she repeated to herself.

When Rana laid eyes on Dallas, she understood Tyrell's reaction. He wore a long-sleeved burgundy tee shirt that hugged his frame divinely, a pair of dark jeans that hung from him like silk, and black boots. Motorcycle boots to be precise.

"Hey," she said, trying to ignore just how damn good Dallas looked.

"Hey, beautiful," he said.

Rana cut a sensitive eye toward Tyrell, who was watching them like an episode of his favorite reality show, along with the mother with her two toddlers browsing in the clay section and pretending not to be admiring Dallas.

In hindsight, maybe she should have met with him in her office to lessen the risk of rumors getting started about her and the newcomer.

Rana's eyes slid briefly to the lime green box in Dallas's hand. "What are you doing here?"

"I know you don't care much for flowers, but I got the impression you really like cupcakes. Mainly because you threatened to stab your sister in the hand with a fork if she claimed the last lemon one at dinner the other day."

Rana's eyes widened. Those were the precise words she'd said to Sadona as they cleaned the kitchen after Sunday dinner. "You heard that?"

Dallas grinned and nodded.

"She does love cupcakes," Tyrell said. When Rana shot him a scowl, he flashed a palm, turned away, and pretended to be arranging the counter display. "Well, you do," he mumbled.

Since, in fact, she did like cupcakes, she accepted the box. "Thank you, but I'm sure you didn't come all the way over here just to bring me these."

"Actually, I didn't."

"Ah, let me guess. You came for this." She fished the check from her back pocket. "Buyer's remorse. I get it," she said, not wanting him to feel bad about having to ask for the check back.

Dallas ignored her outstretched hand. "That's not why I'm here, either. I was hoping I could take you to lunch if you weren't too busy."

"Nope, she's not busy at all."

Rana leveled Tyrell with another sharp glance.

"Well, you're not," he mumbled, and again pretended to be busy.

"Good," Dallas said. Reclaiming the box, he passed it to Tyrell, took Rana's hand, and pulled her toward the exit. "I'll have her back in a couple of hours."

"A couple of hours?" Rana said more to herself than to either of them.

"Keep her as long as you'd like," Tyrell said.

Had Tyrell just traded her like a donkey for cupcakes? Rana's legs locked when her good sense kicked in. "*Wait. Wait.*" She couldn't go carting off with Dallas. "I can't go carting off with you."

"Two hours tops, Rana. Just give me two hours."

"Just give him two hours, boss lady," Tyrell said with a mouthful of *her* cupcakes.

After a moment of consideration, she shrugged. "Okay. But I do have a business to run. Two hours, that's it."

Visually satisfied with his victory, Dallas led her away.

"Don't eat all of my cupcakes, Tyrell," she called back.

"If he does, I'll buy you more," Dallas said.

Outside, Rana scanned the several spaces in front of her store. Dallas must have walked there because she didn't see his SUV anywhere, which meant wherever they were headed couldn't be far.

Dallas stepped down from the sidewalk and stood in front of the sexiest Harley she'd ever seen. When he removed the helmet dangling from the long handlebars, she arched a brow. "Um...whose motorcycle is this?"

"Mine."

His? She'd never seen him on a motorcycle. Of course, that didn't mean he didn't own one. Clearly, he did. She'd never ridden a motorcycle before and wasn't convinced she wanted to do so now. "I don't know about this, Dallas." She eyed the sky. "It smells like rain." Plus, the toe she'd broken several years back suggested it, too.

"Do you see a dark cloud in the sky?"

No, she didn't, but... "I'm not sure—"

"You're in safe hands, Rana. Trust me."

Trust him? She barely knew him. However, something told her she was indeed in safe hands. Besides, this could be fun. Something she hadn't really had in a while. Oh, what the heck. She gave Dallas a slight nod, and he strapped the helmet he'd removed from the motorcycle bag onto her head. Once his was in place, he climbed onto the bike, directing her to climb on behind him.

"Wrap your arms around me," he said over his shoulder.

She did, her body instantly warming from the

feel of him.

"Tighter. You don't want to fall off, right?"

No, she didn't.

Several minutes later they were off. Rana had to admit that she'd been missing out. Now she understood people's fascination with motorcycles. The open countryside, wind whipping across her face... But, by far, the best part of this trip was her arms locked around Dallas. His warm, hard body felt so good.

"You okay back there?"

"Yes," she said, mimicking his high tone. "This is great," she admitted.

"I had a feeling you'd like it."

She chuckled at his sureness. *Confident, but not cocky.*

Roughly forty-five minutes later, they pulled into a gravel lot. *The Polished Diner.* There was no mistaking how the place had gotten its name. You couldn't look directly at the shiny silver building without shielding your eyes. Squinting, Rana said, "Whoa. That's bright."

Dallas helped her off the bike. "I know it doesn't look like much, but trust me, the food is fantastic. Plus, they have a perfect one hundred sanitation grade."

That part seemed to really make him happy.

They moved toward the diner. Rana noticed nearly all of the parking spaces were occupied. A sign that read *country cooking at its finest* was posted in one of the oversized windows.

"Almost an hour outside of town. Do you not want to be seen with me?" Rana smirked, knowing that wasn't the case, but giving Dallas a hard time.

"I don't have an issue with us being seen together, but I believe you do. Are you worried about what people might say?"

"No," she said a little too flimsy to be believable.

He opened the door, and she stepped inside. The interior was outfitted in black and red. The black and white checkerboard flooring made her feel like she'd stepped back in time. Given the fact that the place resembled an oversized sardine can, she'd been sure it would be smoldering. But it wasn't. It was quite comfortable.

"Well, he said he was bringing someone special here," came from behind them.

Rana turned to see a solidly built older black gentleman with a perfectly trimmed and completely gray goatee. His polished bald head shone as brilliantly as the outside of the building.

Someone special? When had she become someone special?

Dallas made the quick introductions. "Rana, Moe. Moe, Rana. Moe owns the place."

Rana stuck out her hand. "Nice to meet you."

"Nice to *finally* meet you," Moe said. "I've heard a lot of nice things about you."

About me? The information stunned her. Apparently, Dallas had mentioned her once or twice. What nice things could he have said? He barely knew her. "Nice things? Really?"

"Sho' nuff," said the silver fox.

"Well, I don't think he was referring to me." She lowered her voice, "Truth be told, I don't even like the big lug."

Moe bellowed in laughter. Sobering, he said, "Uh-oh."

Dallas rested his hand over his heart. "Killing me softly, Moe. She's killing me softly."

Rana smirked, then bumped Dallas playfully. "I'm only kidding." She paused for a moment. "He's kinda growing on me."

***

Dallas led Rana to a free booth near the back of the restaurant. Once she slid in, he lowered to the strip of space she'd left at the end of the black leather bench seat and urged her to move farther inside. "*Schooch*," he said.

Fine lines creased her forehead. "Schooch? What the heck is that?"

"It means scoot your gorgeous ass over so I can get comfortable," he said.

Her gaze slid to the empty space across from them. "Um...you do know there's no one sitting on that side of the booth, right?"

"I can see that, but I want to sit beside you. Is that a problem?" He had a feeling something slick was about to fly out of her beautiful mouth. She obviously reconsidered whatever she was about to say, because a second later she inched over.

He draped his arms over the back of the booth. "See, this isn't so bad, is it?"

Rana's lips parted slightly, then closed.

"Look at these two love birds," Moe said, approaching their booth.

Rana's eyes rose to Moe, her expression unreadable.

"I know what this one here wants," Moe said, resting his hand on Dallas's shoulder, "but what can I get for you, young lady?"

Rana quickly scanned the menu. "I'll have the butter pecan waffle."

"Excellent choice," Moe said.

After taking their drink order, Moe strolled away.

Rana shifted toward Dallas. "What exactly have you been telling Moe?"

"How I met a woman whom I'm very interested in getting to know, but she's playing hard to get. How I can't shake her from my system. How she's trying to hide the fact that she really likes me, too."

Rana eyed him curiously. "I like you?"

"I know."

She barked a laugh. "I wasn't confessing. I was asking—"

"If I wanted to kiss you? Why, yes, I do."

When he tilted his head forward, Rana reeled back. "What do you think you're doing?"

He would have actually been convinced she

was insulted, had her eyes not been fixed on his mouth. "Giving you what you want."

She stared at him for a long moment. "There are plenty of women in Mount Pleasance. Beautiful women. Any number of them would jump at the opportunity to get to know you."

"You're right. There are a lot of beautiful women in Mount Pleasance." It was faint, but he saw her jaw flinch as if him acknowledging that bothered her. "But I want you."

"Because I'm so special?"

Dallas noted the skepticism in her voice. "Truthfully?"

"The truth is always good."

"You fascinate me. I've always gotten what I wanted, Rana. That includes any woman I wanted." A hint of concern spread across her face. Yes, it sounded arrogant, but she'd asked for the truth. He continued, "But not you. You're a challenge. I've never put this much effort into pursuing a woman. And as strange as it seems... I'm actually enjoying the chase. So, yeah, that makes you kinda special."

"Huh," was all she said.

A beat later, Rana's gaze left his. He could tell something troubled her. "What's wrong?" he asked.

"You talk a good game, Dallas. Forgive me if I don't readily fall for any of it. Just because I'm a small town girl, doesn't mean I'll fall for big city smooth talk."

Dallas barked a laugh. "Big city smooth talk?

Damn, woman. Why are you so difficult?"

"Because I loved a man like you once," she snapped. "Charming, handsome, knew exactly what to say and when to say it. I fell for it. I fell for it all. Then all of his lies and promises came crashing down, and I was buried under the rubble. Once I clawed my way out, I swore I'd never let another man bamboozle me again."

Ah. Now he understood. Some creep had hurt her. But she had him all wrong. He didn't play games. Before he could respond, their food arrived at the table. Moe chatted a minute, then left them to their meal. Instead of digging into his Big Poppa breakfast —thick-cut bacon, link sausage, country ham, scrambled eggs, and hash browns—Dallas pushed his plate away and directed his attention back to Rana.

"I'm an original, Rana Lassiter," he said.

In an exhausted voice, she said, "What does that mean, Dallas?"

"It means you've never dealt with a man like me. If you had, you'd still be in love. There's not a man or woman in this room that hasn't been hurt at least once. Including me. Pain is a part of life. We experience it, we learn from it, we eventually get passed it. We don't shut down because we're afraid of the unknown."

Rana's eyes slid away from him and fixed on her double-stacked waffles.

"I don't mean this to sound harsh, but I'm sure the jerk that hurt you is out living and loving again.

Don't allow him to continue robbing you of your happiness. He doesn't deserve that. Just like he didn't deserve you. Let me in, Rana. Let me save you."

Rana's head whipped toward him. Her face scrunched in obvious irritation, as if the idea of a man—any man—saving her was appalling. "Save me? Save me from what?"

"From yourself."

5

Though it had been close to an hour since he'd said them, Dallas's words still rang in Rana's head. *Save me from myself?* As much as she wanted to deny it—and be livid—she couldn't do either. Maybe Dallas had been right. Maybe... *No*. She kicked the absurd notion away, but it crept right back in.

Maybe she was endangering her own happiness by holding on so tightly to her past hurt. Would it be so bad to play the damsel in distress and allow Dallas to ride in on his horse—er Harley—and save her?

The visual of him whipping in, scooping her off her feet, and riding off into the sunset made her laugh. Sobering, her brow bunched. She didn't recall them passing this mile-long white picket fence or all of this farmland. "Dallas, where are we going?"

"A quick detour."

Detour? To her surprise, she didn't feel a desire to protest, just to ride. After several more miles, they turned off the main road. The Harley bounced along the rutted path lined with lush trees on either side. With anyone else, she may have been concerned. Not with Dallas. She felt completely safe. Still, where in the hell was he taking her?

"Oh, my God," she mumbled, stunned by the

picturesque scene that opened up before them once they'd cleared the thatch of trees. Dallas killed the engine, dismounted, then helped her off. "Wow."

Her eager eyes swept the entire area. From the aged structure off in the distance, to the grass as green as fresh paint. A stream cut through the land, flowing along a narrow rock-lined path. Countless pine trees bordered the secluded location. Oh, how she wished she had a canvas, paint, and brushes.

"I thought you'd like it here," Dallas said.

"It's...beautiful."

Dallas removed what resembled a rolled up sleeping bag from the front of the bike. "I thought we'd hang out here for a while." He shrugged. "Talk, take a nap, whatever. Just a little while. Are you okay with that?"

"Yes."

He flashed a lopsided smile. "Good. Why don't you pick the spot to spread the blanket."

"Okay," she said, leading the way to an area a few feet away from the flowing water. "Right here is perfect."

"I agree. Perfect."

She got the feeling they were no longer taking about the location. Dallas spread the nylon backed wool blanket, then guided her down. When he eased down next to her, they were so close their thighs touched. Nervous energy fluttered in her stomach. Or maybe it was the pesky longing she experienced anytime they were this close.

"How did you discover this place?" she asked, ignoring the sensation crawling up her spine.

"Just riding one day." He scrutinized their surroundings. "Something guided me here."

She definitely believed that. No one could have found this place without some kind of cosmic intervention. "Are we trespassing? I really don't want to get shot today."

They shared a laughed that relieved a lot of the tension she'd felt moments earlier.

"I'll protect you," he said.

Something told her he was fully capable of doing so. They eyed one another for a long time. In this natural light, she saw several gray hairs peppering his beard. Oddly, it made him look even sexier. She would have expected to see at least one of two imperfections on his smooth, chocolate face. Nothing. His skin was flawless.

"So, Rana Lassiter, tell me the hardest thing you've ever had to do."

Besides sitting this close to you and resisting the urge to run my hands all over your chiseled body? Of course, she kept that to herself. Rana decided to have a little fun with him, show him she wasn't as hard-nosed as he might think. "Readjusting into society. Everyone inside told me once I got out, it would be hard, but it hasn't been so difficult. My sisters—"

Dallas's flashed his palm. "*Whoa, whoa.* You were in jail?"

His voice rose several octaves, forcing Rana to bite back her laughter. "No."

He blew a sigh of relief. "Whew."

"Prison, actually."

"Pr—" His eyes narrowed in suspicion. "Wh-what did you do? If you don't mind me asking."

Rana studied her fiddling fingers. "My ex..." She paused for effect. "I...I stabbed him. Seventeen times." She buried her face in her hands. "Actually, *I* didn't stab him. It was Brandi. But no one would believe me."

"Brandi? Who's..." He cleared his throat. "Who's Brandi?"

Rana blew out a heavy breath. "One of my alters. But don't worry; as long as I take my meds they don't bother me...much."

Dallas's expression was a mix of concern and utter shock. He stared at her long and hard as if trying to determine his next move. A short time later, he glanced toward the sky. "You know what. I think you were right. It's going to rain. We should..." He scrambled to his feet. "...go. We should get on the road." He was halfway to the motorcycle before he'd finished the sentence.

Standing, Rana called out to him. "What about the blanket?"

"Leave it."

Unable to keep a straight face a second longer, Rana laughed so hard her side hurt. Dallas eyed her from several feet away, concern etching in his face. Clearly, he thought she was having some kind of mental breakdown. He took a couple of steps back, nearly flipping over his motorcycle.

"I'm only kidding, Dallas. You should have seen your face." More laughter poured from her.

"Kidding?"

"Yes, I was just kidding. An icebreaker." She bit back more laughter.

Dallas rested his hands on his hips and glanced to the side. "An icebreaker, huh?" A beat later, he barreled toward her. "I got your icebreaker."

Wide-eyed, she squealed and took off in the opposite direction.

"Oh, you're going to pay for this, woman."

"I'm sorry, I'm sorry," she said, between fits of laughter.

Like kids, they sprinted around the field. When Dallas finally caught her, he scooped her into his arms and threatened to toss her into the water. Rana gasped, clawing at him like a cat.

"You better not, Dallas! It's not my fault you're a chicken."

"Oh, you're still talking smack, huh? Enjoy your swim."

"Okay, okay. I apologize." She sobered. "I apologize."

This time Dallas laughed. "Do you really think I would toss you into the water?"

With her breathing heavy, she said, "Yes, I do. You have that shifty look in your eyes." When her gaze involuntary lowered to her mouth, she craved tasting him. Why did he stir her appetite so much?

"Go ahead. You can kiss me if you want."

"I don't want to kiss you, thank you very much." Which was a total lie, but she couldn't risk their mouths touching in this ultra-romantic setting. She couldn't be held responsible for what could happen afterward.

"Well, I want to kiss you," he said.

"Really? Just a minute ago, you were ready to rush me back to Mount Pleasance. I wasn't so special or desirable when you thought I'd done time in prison, was I?" She shook her head. "Men. All you want is perfect, never flawed. Well, I'm flawed, Dallas. As flawed as they come." She shimmied out of his arms and returned to the blanket.

Dallas joined her. "I couldn't give a damn about your flaws, Rana. We all have flaws. And we all have things that affect us in not-so-good ways. In college, I dated a woman with mental illness. So when you started talking about alters and medication, it took me back to a not-so-good time in my life."

Rana wasn't sure how to respond. All she knew is she felt horrible for dredging up bad memories that clearly still affected him. She wanted to know more but didn't ask him to face the demons of his past.

"Her name was Rhonda. We were juniors. One day she started mumbling to herself. I didn't think much of it. She was pre-med. I just assumed she was reciting parts of the human body or something. But when the mumbles morphed into full-fledged conversations, loud conversations in the middle of the night, I knew something was wrong."

Dallas paused a moment and shook his head. Rana wanted to pull him into her arms and comfort him. Instead, she rubbed his arms to offer her support.

"It was hell, Rana. She would cover all the electronics in aluminum foil because she believed they were omitting signals into outer space. She spray-painted the windows black so the alien death rays couldn't be beamed in. She duct-taped all of the door seals so the poisonous gas coming from the foreign aircraft couldn't seep inside. It got to a point I was actually afraid of her."

Her tone was gentle when she asked, "What did you do?"

He shrugged. "Once I realized she needed more help than I could provide, I contacted her parents and told them something was very wrong. They came, packed her up and took her away. I tried reaching out on several occasion, but it was like she fell off the face of the planet."

"You never saw her again?"

"Several years later, she reached out through social media to say hello. She'd gotten married, had several kids and was doing great. I was genuinely happy to see she'd gotten the help she needed."

"Did you love her?"

He nodded slowly. "Yeah, I did. That experience changed me. And not for the better. I felt completely helpless. I hated that feeling and swore I would never be in a situation like that again. I shut down and refused to allow myself to get close to anyone again."

It didn't surprise her at all that he liked being in control. But she wholeheartedly understood him building a barrier around himself. She'd done the same thing.

Dallas eyed her. "You're the first person I've ever told this story."

"I'm sorry, Dallas. What I did was insensitive. Had I known... Either way, I never should have made light of something as serious as mental illness. Forgive me?"

"There's nothing to forgive, Rana. But if it'll make you happy, I forgive you."

She bumped him playfully. "Thank you."

Dallas's eyes raked over her face as if he were attempting to memorize her features. For a moment, she was sure he was about to lean in and kiss her. He didn't.

"You and your sisters seem really close."

"We are."

"Is it just you three?"

Since he'd shared something personal with her, she decided to share something personal with him. "We had a brother. Phoenix. He took his own life a few years ago. He'd struggled with depression and PTSD."

"I'm sorry. I didn't—"

"It's okay," she said, cutting him off and swallowing the painful lump of emotion forming in the back of her throat. Talking about Phoenix always brought back so much pain. Now was not the time for her to burst out into tears. She flashed a lazy smile. "What about you? Siblings?"

"One brother. Denver."

"Wait. Dallas and Denver?" She laughed. "Really?"

Dallas chuckled. "It was my mother's bright idea to name us after the cities where we were conceived. And, of course, my father went along with it."

"I like your mother already."

"She's as tough as nails. She taught in the inner-city for years. Everyone knew not to try Mrs. Fontaine."

Rana arched a brow. "Your mother was a teacher?"

"Yes. English."

"So was my mother. She also taught English. What a coincidence." For a second, Rana wondered if Gadiya had made Dallas privy to the information and he was now using it to his advantage, but she quickly dispelled the notion because of its ridiculousness.

"How often did you get reprimanded for using improper English?"

Rana tossed her head back in laughter. "All. The. Time."

"Me, too. I still get reprimanded."

If her mother had still been living, the woman would have definitely still been correcting Rana, as well.

Dallas startled her when he plucked a dandelion and placed it behind her ears. "Thank you."

"You know what this means, right?"

"That you don't know the difference between a flower and a weed?"

He chuckled. "You don't like flowers, remember? But that's not what I was referring to. I was referring to the fact that both our mothers were teachers."

"No, I don't think I know what it means." Though she had an idea that whatever he thought it meant would surely make her laugh.

"It means this is destiny."

Yep, she'd been right. "You don't give up, do you?"

"Not easily."

Dallas's eyes lowered to her mouth. She fought the urge to catapult toward him, drape her arms around his neck, and kiss him like a wild woman.

"Earth to Rana."

Rana snapped from her thoughts. "Um, what's your favorite movie?"

His brow knitted. "My favorite movie?"

"Yes. We're getting to know each other, right?"

One side of his mouth lifted. "Yes, we are. But I can't tell you my favorite movie."

He rested back on his elbows. The move caused his shirt to lift slightly, revealing a peep of his toned midsection. Yanking her eyes away, she said, "Why?"

"You'll laugh."

"I won't laugh."

"Oh, you'll laugh."

Now, she had to know. "I won't laugh, Dallas. Really. Pinky swear."

Their gazes held for a moment. By the gleam in his dark eyes, she should have known she would regret what would come flying out of his mouth next.

"Let it be known, if you laugh, I'm going to kiss you."

The stern expression on his face told her he was dead serious. Could she take that kind of risk? What was the big deal? She could hold her laughter. *How bad could it be?* "I won't laugh." A beat later, Dallas mumbled something she couldn't quite make out. "I didn't catch that. Repeat, please. And this time...a little louder."

"The Lion King," he said.

"As in...the *Disney* movie?"

He nodded. "You better not laugh."

Rana bit at the corner of her lip. Oh, she was wrong. Sooo wrong. When her lip twitched, she bit down harder. *Don't laugh. Don't laugh*. A second later, she slapped her hand over her mouth to muffle her amusement. And without skipping a beat, Dallas removed her hand and kissed her deliciously.

And she kissed him back.

Hungrily.

Greedily.

Shamelessly.

His warm tongue explored every inch of her mouth. When she sucked it gently, a beautiful sound rumbled in his chest. Yeah, he liked this just as much as she did. Somehow, he managed to maneuver onto his knees without breaking their mouths apart.

He glided her back until she was laying flat on the blanket. His hardness pressed against her. This time it didn't scare her, but caused the throb in her core to intensify. Her nipples beaded so tightly inside her bra they hurt. Her entire body ignited and threatened to turn her to ashes.

They kissed long and hard, slow and gentle, impatient and raw. By the time he pulled away, her lips were kiss-swollen and achy, but she had no complaints.

Dallas stared down into her face. "You may not believe me, but I didn't bring you out here for this."

She wasn't a hundred percent convinced of that. "Then why did you bring me to the middle of nowhere?"

"To get to know you."

"I'm giving you an opportunity to *really* get to

know me."

He studied her. "Is that what you really want, Rana? Some meaningless screw in the grass?"

Yes, she screamed in her head. It had been way too long since she'd had sex. Her body needed this. Why couldn't they have sex now and sort things out later?

She laughed at herself. Wasn't it usually the man who worked to get in the woman's pants, not the other way around? There was no shame in her game. She wanted what she wanted. And, at the moment, that was Dallas.

"It's just sex, Dallas."

"No, it's not. When we make love, baby, I want it to mean something. I want it to be so special that you feel like all of your shattered pieces are coming back together."

Rana wasn't completely sure how to take Dallas. She'd never encountered a man like him. So sure. So confident. So determined...to have her in his life. Not that she thought she wasn't worthy of his advances, she just needed to know one thing. "Why me, Dallas?"

"Woman, you give off this incredible energy. I don't know if anyone else can feel it, but I can. I like it. I want to be a part of it."

A smile curled her lips. "You're all types of trouble, you know that?"

Dallas smirked, pecked her gently, then rolled back to a sitting position. Rana followed suit.

"Tell me about your ex," he said.

"My ex?"

"Yes."

"How does me telling you about him help you get to know me?"

"Because if you tell me he didn't listen enough, wasn't romantic enough, couldn't satisfy you like you wanted and needed to be satisfied...that tells me a whole lot."

Walton hadn't listened enough, and he definitely hadn't been romantic enough. But he'd been okay in bed. However, she didn't want to discuss any of this with Dallas. "I prefer *not* to talk about him if that's okay with you."

Dallas smiled. *"Hmm."*

"Hmm. What does that mean?"

"Your not wanting to talk about him also tells me a whole lot."

"Like?"

"That you're over him. If you weren't, you would have jumped at the opportunity to bash him, which would have possibly meant you were still holding onto some repressed anger."

"A philosophizing fireman."

"I'm full of surprises."

Oh, she bet he was. Sending her gaze straight ahead, Rana inched her hand closer to Dallas's and looped her finger over his. It was a start. "I have a confession. I've never ridden a motorcycle before."

Dallas rested a hand on his chest and gasped. "You don't say."

Rana snickered at the animated expression on

his face. "What gave it away?"

"The reluctance at your shop, for one. Rain? Was that the only excuse you could come up with?"

"Trust me, it's going to rain. Just you wait and see, buddy."

He eyed her skeptically. "Uh-huh."

"Okay, unbeliever. What else gave it away?"

"How tightly you held on to me. Though, I suspect that had nothing to do with the motorcycle at all. I think you just enjoyed having your arms around me."

"Don't flatter yourself, lover boy."

"You want me to teach you to ride?"

"Ha! And break my neck? No, thank you."

Dallas pushed to his feet and held out his hand for her to take. "You won't break your neck. I won't let you. We'll go as slow as you need to go."

The latter statement felt as if it held dual meaning. After a few moments of considering his offer, she placed her hand into his. The reaction to his touch was instant with a sizzling hot heat racing up her arm. Once on her feet, Dallas pulled her closer to him. If she didn't know any better, she'd have believed he enjoyed torturing her.

"Do you feel that?"

Heck, she was feeling a lot of things, so she needed him to be a little more specific. "Feel what, exactly?"

"That spark that happens every time we touch."

Rana flashed a devilish smirk. "No," she said, then playfully pushed him away. "Get over yourself, Dallas Fontaine." Strolling toward his motorcycle, she tossed over her shoulder, "You are not every woman's dream."

He rushed up behind her and wrapped his strong arms around her waist. "That's perfectly okay with me, because I just want to be one woman's dream. I know I come on strong, but I've never been a man to allow a good thing pass me by. With that said, I'm going to break your code, Rana Lassiter. And I'm going to have fun doing it."

Why shouldn't she have a little fun, too?

By the time they made it back to town, it was well past seven in the evening. *So much for two hours tops*.

Since she usually walked to work, there was no reason to return to the shop. Dallas pulled into her driveway, cut the engine and removed his helmet. "I won't invite myself in. I'm sure you've had your fill of me for one day. Literally," he said with a sly grin. "I'll walk you to the door."

"That's not necessary," she said, dismounting from the bike. Passing Dallas her head gear, she said, "Thank you for today."

"Did you have fun?"

As hard as it was to admit, she said, "Today was fantastic."

Dallas arched a brow. "*Fantastic?* That means a brother must have done something right. It was the motorcycle lesson, wasn't it?"

"Well, it certainly wasn't the hour we had to sit under the overpass because you didn't believe me when I said it was going to rain."

While they'd waited for the showers to pass, they'd talked about everything. His career, her passion for painting, their childhoods. They'd laughed. They'd shared comfortable silence.

He groaned. "Did I lose brownie points for that?"

"No. Your brownie points are still intact."

"Good. So, does that mean I get to see you again? This time on an official date."

Rana hugged one arm around her waist, then used the other to massage the back of her neck. "I need a minute to process this, Dallas. To process you. A part of me is saying to let this happen, but another part of me is saying to run like hell from you. I know I'm being wishy-washy and am sending mixed signals, and I totally get it if you toss your hands up and want nothing more to do with me. I hope you don't do that, but I need to do this at my own pace. This is—"

"*Shh,*" Dallas hissed, cutting her off. His brow furrowed. "Do you hear that?"

Her ears perked. "I don't hear—"

"Listen closely."

Rana glanced around, straining against the silence. Tuning out the sounds of nature, she said, "Yeah, I do hear something. What is it?"

Dallas hooked his arm around her waist and brought her close. "That's the sound of you falling for me."

He brought his mouth close to hers, but he didn't kiss her. Instead, he nudged her playfully in an attempt to get her to make the first move. Shamelessly, she did, pressing her lips against his.

That was all it took.

Dallas kissed her in a manner that urged her to ignore all the doubt swirling around in her head. Her body ignited from his touch, just as it had earlier. Only this time, an inferno raged inside of her. Thankfully, Dallas possessed enough strength to pull away. If it had been up to her, they'd have remained in this same spot all night tasting and tempting each other.

"I didn't put all of this energy into you just to let you slip right through my fingers. I get your hesitation. You need a man to show you he'll be yours and only yours. A man to make you a priority in his life. A man to show you how it can and should be done."

That certainly sounded like a good start.

Dallas released her and slid his helmet back on. When he started the motorcycle, the vibration further aggravated the throbbing between her legs.

In a high voice, he said, "I'm that man, Rana Lassiter. You're going to be mine, sweet lady. Take all the time you need to process that."

Damn, he certainly didn't mince words, did he? "We'll talk soon," she said. "Drive safely." She turned and headed toward the house.

"Hey."

She shifted toward him again.

"If there's ever a choice between fear and happily-ever-after...always choose happily-ever-after." He winked, popped the bike in gear and took off.

Fear, doubt, and experience all screamed run like hell. But in that moment, her heart calmly said stay put and let this happen.

6

Dallas let go of the pull-up bar when Nico entered the workout room inside the fire station. He chuckled when Nico assessed him with a strange look, folding his arms across his chest and narrowing his eyes at Dallas. This was a sure sign something was up.

"What?" Dallas asked.

"You tell me. Every night this week, my wife has been on the phone with her sisters until nearly one in the morning."

"How do you know it has something to do with me?"

"Because you and Rana have been on a date every night this week and last. Plus, every time I walk into the room, Gadiya clams up and gives me the stank-eye."

Dallas chuckled. Yeah, they'd definitely been discussing him. Moving to the weight bench, he eased down. "I know it's only been a little while, but I'm crazy about your sister-in-law, man."

"From what I gather, she's pretty crazy about you, too. I don't know what kind of voodoo dust you're sprinkling, but whatever it is, it's working. I haven't seen Rana this happy in a while. You two deserve each other. It's kinda freaky, though."

"What's that?"

"Watching the infamous Dallas Fontaine

falling so hard for a woman. A small-town woman at that. But hey, I warned you. That Lassiter woman magic is real and potent."

There just might have been some truth to Nico's magic claim. Dallas couldn't stop thinking about Rana. Even when he was *not* trying to think about her, she'd find a way to invade his thoughts, making it impossible to concentrate on much of anything else but her.

Nico stood above Dallas, spotting him. "Have you told her you're worth a mint, yet?"

"Nah, not yet." Dallas had every intention of telling Rana about his family's wealth. But for now, he just wanted her to know him as Dallas Fontaine, Mount Pleasance firefighter. Not Dallas Fontaine, heir to a fortune. In a strained voice, he said. "But soon. I want to take her to Washington in a few weeks. Meet my mom." It had been years since he'd introduced a woman to his mother. No doubt she would like Rana as much as he did.

"Damn. This is serious, huh?"

Yes, it was. It wasn't like him to drop his guard so easily, because he was always suspicious of the women he encountered. One question always presented itself: were they interested in him or his money? Most often, it was the latter and the perks that came along with dating him. It wasn't like that with Rana. To her, he was just an average Joe trying to woo her. He wanted to hold on to that as long as he could.

"Daydreamer, you with me?" Nico said.

Dallas refocused on their conversation. "I'm here. I'm here. Speaking of serious, who was the woman feeling you up this morning and trying to spoon feed you banana pudding?"

Nico groaned. "Mrs. Augustine. She's a lovely lady, but whatever you do, don't *ever, ever, ever* eat any of her banana pudding. *Ever*." Nico shivered. "She'll tell you it's to die for and you'll come very close to doing just that. Plus, she has like thirty cats."

Dallas grimaced. "Thanks for the heads-up."

Nico snapped his fingers. "Shit, I almost forgot why I came in here. I already told the other guys. Mark your calendar. Everyone has to have their annual physical complete and on file. You have two months."

"Cool." He was overdue for a physical anyway. When Dallas's cell phone rang, he returned the weighted bar to its resting place. Fishing the phone from his pocket, he smiled at the screen. "I have to take this, man," then excused himself.

"Tell Rana I said what's up."

"Hey, Mom," Dallas said into the line. "Is everything okay?"

"Hi, son. Yes, everything is fine. I just wanted to hear your voice. It feels like an eternity since I've seen you. You'll be coming for a visit soon, I hope. Introduce me to that young lady you keep going on and on about." She didn't give Dallas a chance to respond before shooting off a missile of questions. "How are you? Do you need anything? Are you eating decent meals?"

Sometimes he believed his mother forgot he was a grown man and no longer a dirty-behind-the-ears boy. But he loved the concern she always showed for both him and Denver. "Yes, I'm fine. No, I don't need anything. And I'm probably eating too much."

"You know I worry about my boys. No matter how old you get. That's part of a mother's job, to worry."

"Yes, ma'am. I know. But I'm perfectly fine. You don't have to worry your pretty little self about me." Which was just like telling his mother not to breath.

A beat of silence played on the opposite end. Finally, his mother said, "I spoke with Denver earlier. His lip is still poked out a mile. He misses you something awful. He's determined to get you back to Washington."

Dallas and Denver had always been thick as thieves. From jump, his brother had hated the idea of him moving away. And when the decision had officially been made, he'd verbally protested, all but forbidding him to go. Like he was the older brother and not Dallas.

Dallas had known the move would be good for them both. It would give him the opportunity to reinvent himself, and it would give Denver a chance to chart his own path without the influence of his big brother. Of course, Denver knew if he ever needed him, he was only a phone call away.

His mother's soft voice pulled him back to the conversation.

"Denver needs to find himself a nice young lady to settle down with. Lord, I love that son of mine, but he is such a rascal."

Dallas barked a laugh. He was sure what his mother really wanted to say was that her youngest son was a whore, which would have been a hundred percent accurate. As scandalous as Dallas had been in his younger years, Denver was ten times worse. Dallas took some of the blame. He hadn't always been the best role model.

"He'll—" Before he could finish his thought, a station alert sounded. "I have to go, Mom. Love you," he said, ending the call.

Like lightening, Dallas slid into his turnout gear. Something about the address that had been dispatched to them rang familiar. Then it hit him. It was Rana's address. Adrenaline coursed through his veins, and he willed the twenty-ton vehicle to move faster. His heart pounded in his chest. He didn't need this kind of excitement at ten in the morning.

When they arrived on the scene, he took the fact that he hadn't seen any smoke or flames as a good sign. The truck hadn't come to a complete stop before he was out and racing across the yard. Ignoring all of his training, he banged on the front door. *"Rana! Rana!"*

The front door swung open, and he rushed inside. The smell of charred food instantly filled his nose. Rana appeared frazzled in the oversized white nightshirt she wore, but otherwise, unharmed. Still, he gave her a once-over. "What happened? Are you okay?"

Rana rested her hand on her forehead and groaned. "Yes. It's a false alarm. I tried to contact the alarm company, but it was too late. I'm sorry."

"Hold on a sec." Dallas waved the other guys back to the engine. "False alarm." Returning back inside, he said, "What did you burn?"

She pouted. "My last box of macaroni and cheese. It's all your fault."

His brow arched. "My fault?"

"Yes. You keep my creative juices flowing. I was in my studio painting and forgot the pasta was boiling. You owe me a pot."

He laughed, then kissed her forehead. Draping his arms around her, he said, "I'll buy you a hundred pots. Just don't scare me like that again, okay?" When she nodded, he placed a finger under her chin, tilted her head, and pecked her gently. "I have to go. I'll see you tonight."

"Okay. Sorry again for the false alarm. Tell Nico he better not fine me."

"False alarm, huh? I think you just wanted to see me."

Rana smirked. "I'll never tell."

"Let me get out of here before you get me in trouble." He winked, then walked away.

"Hey, Mr. Fireman," Rana called out to him.

Dallas turned.

"You're looking awfully sexy in that getup." This time, she winked, then closed the door.

Yep, he was a goner.

***

Rana fell against the closed door and swooned. Nearly burning down her kitchen hadn't been intentional, but she couldn't deny she'd benefitted from the mishap. There was nothing like a sexy fireman. *Her* sexy fireman. That brought a smile to her face.

She still hadn't gotten completely used to the idea that she and Dallas were officially dating. After much resistance, she'd given in. Things had moved so fast with them, and maybe it had been poor judgment to fall for him so soon, but she'd been powerless against it. He was truly unlike any other man she'd ever known.

Was she crazy? *Maybe*. But being with him felt right. Everything about their relationship felt right. Everything about Dallas felt…right. Had she ever been so content in a relationship? *No*.

Pushing away from the door, she ventured into the kitchen, lifting the ruined pot. "No amount of vinegar and baking soda is going to help this." Tossing the cookware into the garbage, she pilfered the fridge, claiming a couple slices of deli turkey. She really needed to go grocery shopping.

When her cell phone rang, she lifted it from the counter and checked the caller ID. *Private*.

Typically, she didn't answer blocked numbers but made an exception this time. Seeing her beau had put her in a jolly mood.

Unfortunately, her shiny disposition ended the second the caller's voice raked over the line—and her nerves.

"Hello, Rana."

In a level tone, she said, "Walton." She hadn't heard from her ex in close to a year and couldn't imagine why he'd be contacting her now. "What can I do for you?"

"I thought you'd want to know my mother passed today."

The news stilled Rana and tugged at her heartstrings. She'd always thought very highly of Walton's mother. On many occasions, the woman had told her she had been the best thing to ever happened to her son. Rana regretted not keeping in contact with her after her breakup with Walton.

"I'm sorry for your loss, Walton." She genuinely felt some degree of sympathy for him, because she knew how close he was to his mother. The only boy in a house full of women.

"Thank you. I figured you'd want to attend the service. Mom really loved you, you know?"

Rana could hear the emotion in Walton's voice. He may have been a sorry excuse for a man, but he had always been a great son. She couldn't take that away from him.

"You will come, won't you?"

Rana hated funerals with a passion but felt the

need to pay her respects to the woman who had always referred to her as her daughter-in-law. "Send me the details."

"I will."

The line went silent. For a second, Rana assumed Walton had disconnected. Just as she was about to do the same, he spoke.

"It's good hearing your voice, Ra."

Too bad she couldn't say the same. "I have to go, Walton."

"Oh. Okay. Well, I'll see you—"

She ended the call before he could complete his sentence. The last thing she wanted to do was spend any amount of time with Walton, but she could tolerate him out of respect for Ms. Hedda.

Several hours later, Rana put the finishing touches on her outfit. Dallas had called earlier that day to say he'd be late. If she had her way, they'd spend the evening in, cuddling and watching The Hallmark Channel. Actually, if she really had her way, they'd spend the evening making love.

Fat chance. She totally got that Dallas wanted to take things slow and get to know each other before introducing sex into the mix, but a girl had needs. Desperate desires. Heck, how much more did she need to know about him, anyway?

The doorbell rang, prematurely ending her pity-party. After one last glance in the mirror, she headed out the bedroom. Dallas looked divine in a black Henley shirt and a pair of dark brown slacks. The man truly made any look appear regal. She stepped aside and allowed him in.

Her eyes lowered to the bags he carried. “What’s all of this?”

“Dinner. I thought I’d cook for you since I’m crazy late.”

Rana trailed him into the kitchen. “You’re going to cook for me?”

He placed the bags on the counter. “If that’s okay. You sound surprised.”

“It’s not that. It’s just that…” She flashed a lazy smile. “No man has ever cooked for me before.”

Dallas hooked an arm around her waist and brought her flush against him. “I like the idea of being your first.” He pressed his lips to hers, kissed her gently, then pulled away.

Such a tease. “I have an important question, Dallas.”

“Okay.”

“Can you actually cook or are you experimenting.”

Dallas barked a laugh. “You’d be surprised at the amazing things I can do.”

Somehow, she doubted she’d be surprised at all. Dallas took a step back, his roaming gaze caressing her like curious fingers.

“You look gorgeous. Are you sure you don’t want to go out?”

“And miss this opportunity?”

“I was hoping you would say that.” He pointed to the table. “Take a seat and be prepared to be astonished.”

"Are you sure you don't want me—"

"Woman, sit."

She saluted him. "Sir, yes, sir." Rana considered changing out of the black off-the-shoulder dress into something more comfortable but decided to keep it on when she recalled how Dallas had admired her in it. Kicking off her black heels, she did as instructed.

For the next hour, Rana gleefully watched Dallas work his magic. By the way he handled himself, he was no stranger in the kitchen. His moves were impressive. But that wasn't the only thing that impressed her.

"Hey."

Her eyes dart upward.

"Are you checking me out?"

"I plead the fifth."

He flashed her a dazzling smile, then returned to his task.

"Dallas...can I ask you something? Something personal? Something that's been bothering me."

Eyeing her with a look of concern, he said, "What is it?"

"It's none of my business, really. But like I said, it's been bothering me. And I usually don't meddle in—"

"Rana." He laughed. "Out with it already. I'm—"

"Where did you get the twenty-five thousand dollars you gave me?" She bit at the corner of her lip, hoping she hadn't overstepped.

Dallas shifted away from her and stirred one of the steaming pots. "I...um..."

"I'll never lie to you, Dallas. Please don't lie to me."

A second later, he turned the stove off and faced her again. Seeing the distress etched in his features, she got worried. Was he embarrassed to admit how he'd gotten it? Had he done something senseless to get it? "I still have the check, Dallas. I'll return it to you. You can keep the paintings."

"I don't need it, Rana. My family has a little money."

"A little?"

"A lot more than a little. A whole lot more."

"Oh. So, you're trying to tell me you're rich."

He folded his arms across his chest and nodded.

"I see." A beat later, Rana burst out laughing. Standing, she trudged toward him. "Come here, my *rich* and super hot fireman." She grabbed his ears and guided his mouth to hers, pecking him several times. "Okay, Million Dollar Dallas, when do we eat? I'm starving."

Dallas pulled his cell phone from his pocket, tapped it several times and passed it to her. The amusement faded as she read about the Washington Fontaines. According to the article, Dallas's family owned the largest medical supply company in the country, valued at over a billion dollars. *A billion*, she repeated in her head. *He wasn't exaggerating*.

Bringing her gaze up slowly, she said. "Wow. You really are rich, huh?" She backed away and leaned her backside against the counter, unsure how to react to the news. This revelation shouldn't have bothered her, but it did.

"This doesn't change anything, Rana."

She released a single laugh. "Ah, yeah, it kinda does, Dallas."

He posted against the counter directly across from her. "Okay." His brows bunched. "What does it change?"

"It— Well—" She huffed and rolled her eyes away, unable to offer a viable response. If he hadn't put her on the spot, she'd have been able to come up with plenty.

"I'm waiting."

She slid a narrow-eyed gaze in his direction. Most men with money—especially Fontaine-type money—were pompous, arrogant, egotistical, overly-confident. But honestly, none of those things described Dallas. Well, maybe the over-confident label could possibly be applied.

In her head, she sighed. Was she overreacting? Dallas hadn't exactly tried to use his financial status as a lure. Besides, it wouldn't have worked. She couldn't care less about how much he was worth. Money didn't entice her. Unfortunately, the Dallas she'd gotten to know did.

Dallas pushed off the counter, closed the distance between them and pressed his warm, hard body against her. Bracing his hands on either side of the counter—to keep her from escaping, she suspected—he watched her in silence. When she turned her head away from him, he placed a hand under her chin and directed it back.

After several moments of silent observation had ticked by, Rana grew impatient. "Are we just going to stand here all night?"

"You're so damn beautiful when you're angry."

"I'm not angry." She lowered her eyes. "I'm scared," she mumbled, instantly regretting how much she'd just revealed.

"Of what?" When she didn't respond, Dallas said, "Look at me, Rana."

Her gaze slowly rose. Why was he so damn alluring?

"What are you afraid of?"

"I don't fit into your world."

"You are my world."

"Stop it, Dallas. Stop making it sound as if in the extremely short time we've been together I've impacted your life in such a way that you can tell me I'm your world. And with a straight face. Just stop it." She tried to push him away, but he didn't budge. "Please move."

"No," was all he said.

"Let's just end this now, Dallas. Before..." Her words trailed. What she couldn't say was before she fell any farther for him.

"Is that what you really want, Rana? To end us?"

She glanced away again. No, it wasn't. "When I fall, I fall hard, Dallas. I don't want my heart broken again." Bringing her eyes back to him, she continued, "Especially not by you, because..."

"Because, what?"

"Because I really like you." Well, if, by chance, they were playing some kind of game, she'd just dealt him the winning hand.

Dallas smiled. "I've been waiting to hear you admit that out loud." He studied her for a moment. "Nothing will change. Not the way I smile when I hear your voice. Not the way my heart skips a beat when I see you. Not the way my temperature rises when we touch. Nothing changes, Rana. Not my need to kiss you. Not my desire to make love to you every damn second of the day. *Nothing*."

Dallas's mouth was so close his bottom lip brushed hers. His beautiful confession kicked her pulse rate up a notch or two. Her breathing grew heavy and sporadic. "Do you have the desire to make love to me now?"

"It is a second and a day."

The idea made her giddy, but the sentiment faded the second she considered one thing. "But you won't because we're taking things slow, right?"

Dallas sighed. "I've come to the realization that taking things slow works best for ordinary couples."

"So, what are we?"

"We're extraordinary, baby."

7

Dallas pressed his lips to Rana's. The kiss started off calm and gentle, but quickly erupted into something full of heat and passion. Tangling his fingers in her hair, he held her mouth close to his. Their tongues searched with urgency. The swell in his pants pressed against his zipper. He couldn't go another day without knowing how it felt to be inside her. "I want to make love to you, Rana. Right now." His pleading tone revealed his desperation, but he didn't give a damn.

"What are you waiting for?" she said.

Something dark settled over him when he considered the magnitude of pleasure he planned to dispense. Hoisting her into his arms, he headed toward the bedroom. Once there, he undressed her nice and slow, then guided her down onto the mattress.

"Damn, you're gorgeous."

"Wait, we shouldn't do this, Dallas."

Urgent concern flushed his body, and he was sure Rana had seen the distress on his face.

A beat later, she smirked. "Gotcha."

He blanketed her body. "Woman, you had me the second I laid eyes on you. But you will pay for this." He kissed her tenderly. His skin prickled from the anticipation of making love to her. When he ground his erection against her, she whimpered.

"Get used to making that sound," he said, peppering kisses along her jawline and to the delicate spot below her earlobe. "Do you want me, Rana? As badly as I want you?"

"Yes," she said, the longing in her tone unmistakable.

"Say it," he said, nipping her neck.

"I want you, Dallas. I want—" She sucked in a sharp breath when he sucked her nipple between his lips and flicked it with the tip of his tongue. "I want you. I want you so bad."

Kissing a line to her opposite breast, he gave it equal attention. Cupping them both in his hands, he manipulated them gently as he kissed and nipped his way down her body.

"*Mmmm*," she hummed.

His hands left her breasts, glided down her ribcage and along her soft thighs. Using them to spread her folds, he planted his face in her wetness and ate her like he hoped she'd never been eaten before.

His movements weren't fast or slow, more of a steady tempo. Each lick, flick, twirl of his tongue was meant to deliver pure pleasure and bring her closer and closer to her breaking point. Her legs trembled slightly, and when he curled two fingers inside her and worked them with targeted precision, she came undone.

Rana's back bucked off the mattress, her cries tearing through the room. "*Dallas*."

Her hands came to rest on the back of his

head, holding him in place. If her thighs tightened any more, she would crack his skull. Never veering from her center, he pried her legs open.

"Oh, God!" she screamed a second time, her hips lifting.

He continued to work his tongue, determined to consume every drop of her.

***

Rana was sure Dallas was good at anything he put his mind to. Now, she also knew he was good at anything he put his *mouth* to as well. Of course, she should have already known that by the way he kissed.

When she finally freed him, he snapped out of his clothes. He wasn't at all bashful about his nakedness. Probably because he knew how impressive his body was. Especially his erection. Long, thick and a treat to look at.

Her eyes slowly crawled up his magnificent frame. There wasn't an ounce of fat on him. His midsection was so perfectly ripped, it looked artificial. Looking at his muscular arms made her bite at the corner of her lip in anticipation of them bending and twisting her to his will.

When Rana met his gaze, he smirked and gave her one of those sexy winks. Dallas dug in his pants pocket, removed his wallet and retrieved a condom. "Let me," she said, reaching for the foil. Dallas flashed a look that was a mix of surprise and satisfaction. From his reaction, she concluded not many women had ever volunteered to sheath him before.

Taking him into her hands, she caressed him. Unable to resist the desire to taste him, she took him into her mouth. Using the tip of her tongue, she teased his head. A deep grunt came from somewhere deep in his chest.

"Damn, woman," he said through clenched teeth. "*Mmm*. Your mouth feels amazing. Too amazing." He captured her head between his hands. "Which is why you have to stop."

Guiding her away, he snagged the unopened condom, tore into it and slid it on. A second later, he had her on her back again. This was the moment she'd been waiting for. Unfortunately, he didn't give her what she wanted. Instead, he eyed her as if he were having second thoughts.

"What's wrong?"

"You're wreaking havoc on me, woman. Not just now, but from the first time we met. I've never fallen so hard, so fast. I'm open and exposed with you."

"Does that scare you?"

"Do I strike you as a man who scares easily?"

Before she could answer, Dallas inched her legs apart with his knees. Lowering his head, he kissed her tenderly, sensually, passionately. When he filled her, she moaned into his mouth. A thousand sensations invaded her all at once. The pleasure was so intense it made her dizzy.

Dallas broke their connection. "I've imagined this moment a thousand times, baby, but I never dreamed you would feel this damn good."

She wanted to respond, but the words stuck in the back of her throat. All she could do was close her eyes and feel. His slow, steady strokes hit a sweet spot each time he buried himself inside her. He kissed each of her closed lids, her cheek, then the delicate space below her lobe.

Positioning his mouth close to her ear, he whispered, "I'm going to drain you, woman. And when you're completely empty, I'm going to replenish you, then drain you again."

Dallas's wordplay aroused her even more. "Please, Dallas."

He peppered kisses along the column of her neck. "Please what, baby? Do it harder? Do it faster? What? Tell me what you want."

"*Mmm*. All of it. I want all—"

He drove into her with one single, powerful thrust. Her cries ripped through the room. "Yes! Oh, God, yes!"

"You like that?"

"I like it. I like it a lot. Give me more. Give me—" He drove into her again. If she were glass, she'd have been in a million pieces right now. Not because of his force, but because of the pressure built up inside of her. She desperately needed a release. "Make me come, Dallas. I need to come."

"You will. Numerous times, I promise. But our first time together is not going to be a race to the finish line. *Nooo*. I'm going to cherish being inside of you for as long as I can. And when I'm convinced I can't hold back another second, we're going to cross together. Slow and steady wins the race."

"O-okay," she said, because what else, really, could she say? However, she didn't believe for one second she would last much longer.

Dallas covered her mouth again, kissing her like her mouth was the key to his survival. Her hands glided over his damp skin. His forearms, biceps, shoulders, along his ribcage. The feel of his hot flesh under her fingertips sent waves of excitement through her. And just when she thought it couldn't get any better, he rotated his hips in a circular motion.

Dallas drew his mouth away from hers. "Can you feel me, baby?"

"All through my body."

A sound Rana took as gratification rumbled in Dallas's chest. Was he as close to exploding as she was? A hand rested behind one of her knees, and he adjusted her leg, causing him to go even deeper.

Her nails dug into his back with little regard to whether or not it would cause pain. "Dallas!"

He kissed her collarbone. "I'm here, baby. I'm right here, but I'm losing my grip. You feel too damn good. I knew you would."

Rana couldn't hold back a second longer. The release snatched her breath away. All her muscles seized and, for a moment, the intensity of the orgasm took sight and sound from her. Arching off the mattress, she rode the great wave of pleasure. And just when her body started to relax, the feel of Dallas's powerful release sent her over the edge again.

A growl-like moan blasted past his lips as he drove in and out of her. Him throbbing inside of her felt so good she thought she would black out. After several more clumsy strokes, he collapsed next to her. Catching his breath, he maneuvered onto his back and pulled her still trembling body onto his chest. She rose and fell with his still erratic breathing.

"That was..." She didn't have any words to begin to fully encompass how wonderful this experience had been.

"Amazing," Dallas said.

That was a good start.

Several hours later, Rana woke in the same position she'd fallen asleep in after their last round of lovemaking. She eyed the clock. *4:27*. Freeing herself from Dallas's arms, he stirred but didn't wake. Easing from the bed, she grimaced from the stiffness in her joints.

He hadn't lied about draining and replenishing her. The man had proven to be insatiable. And she'd enjoyed every round with him. Every time she'd assumed he'd gotten his fill of her, he'd come back for more, making her feel pretty damn irresistible.

Moving into the bathroom, she handled her business, washed her hands, slid into a nightshirt and journeyed into the kitchen. Dallas had satisfied one craving, now she needed to satisfy another—the growling monster in her stomach.

Instead of reheating the abandoned meal, she swirled one of the seared scallops in the cream sauce and popped it into her mouth. "That's good." She sampled a small bit of everything he'd prepared: steak, green beans, and a cheese polenta dish that melted in her mouth. The man was certainly talented in and out of the bedroom.

Moving to the freezer, she removed her half-eaten container of rum raisin ice cream. *Gotta have dessert.* Spooning a heap of the sweetness into her mouth, she closed her eyes and moaned deeply. "*Mmm.*"

"You keep that up you're going to make me jealous."

Rana turned, her eyes appreciating the sight of Dallas wearing nothing but a pair of dark gray fitted boxers. The imprint pressed against the snug fabric made her giddy. Leaning against the counter, her gaze climbed his lofty frame. "Has anyone ever told you how damn spectacular your body is."

He gave a casual shrug. "Once or twice."

She set the container down and wrapped her arms around Dallas's waist when he pinned her body against the counter. Lowering his head, he kissed her gently. He tasted like sweet mint. *Mouthwash*.

Pulling away, he rested his forehead against hers. "Good morning, beautiful."

"Good morning, handsome. Are you hungry?"

"Starving."

"I'll heat you a plate."

"Oh, you meant was I hungry for food."

She laughed. "Haven't you had enough of me, yet?"

"Is that a trick question?"

When Dallas hoisted her onto the counter, she squealed. "That's cold."

A roguish grin spread across his face. "You're not wearing underwear."

"Didn't think I would need them."

"You were right."

His hands glided up her thighs, giving her goose bumps. She couldn't explain it, especially when she'd fought so hard—well, hard-ish—against it, why this man made her constantly picture the possibilities. "I'm open and exposed with you, too, Dallas. I won't lie and say I like the feeling, but I'm starting to appreciate it."

Cradling her head in his hands, he crushed his mouth to hers and kissed the hell out of her. He hoisted her into his arms, and she instinctively wrapped her legs around him. As they started for the bedroom, Dallas stopped, backtracked, and grabbed the ice cream off the counter.

Something told her she was about to be put into a very sticky situation.

8

Dallas hated the twenty-four-hour shifts he occasionally had to pull at the fire station. Mainly because when he was sleeping there, he wasn't sleeping with Rana. At eleven at night, he should have been asleep, but he couldn't stop thinking about Rana.

Pulling out his cell phone, he scrolled through the gallery, stopping at a picture of the two of them acting silly and making ridiculous faces. *This was rum raisin night*, he reminded himself. Almost a week ago. When he recalled painting Rana's body with the ice cream, then licking it off, he stirred below the waist.

As if he conjured her up with his thoughts, he received an incoming message:

Are you asleep?

No. Laying here thinking about you. There are a few things I'd like to be doing to you right now.

A surprise-face emoji came through.

Do tell. NVM. Keep me in suspense.

A winking smiley face followed.

I wish I were there with you, beautiful. Doing those few things I mentioned earlier.

LOL! I wish you were here, too. Go into the bathroom, strip, stand in front of the mirror and send me a selfie.

Dallas barked a laugh at the request.

I'm a grown man. I don't send dick pics.

Pretty please.

I'm not that guy.

Sad-face emoji.

You're no fun.

I think you know how much fun I can be.

He added a winking emoji before hitting send.

Yes, I do. I'm about to go to sleep and dream about all of that fun. GN. Dream about me, too.

No doubt.

He tossed his phone aside, determined to fall asleep. Fluffing his pillows, he snuggled under the covers. Just when he'd nearly drifted off, he thought about the fact Rana would be going to Charlotte in the morning to attend funeral services for her ex's mother. His eyes popped open.

Folding his arms behind his head, he stared at the ceiling. Why did the idea of her going bother him so much? It wasn't like he was a jealous man. And if he thought he couldn't trust Rana, he wouldn't be with her.

So, what was it? He laughed at the possibility that came to mind. *Fear. Yeah, right.* He'd never been insecure in a relationship. But he'd also never felt about a woman the way he felt about Rana. The more he thought about it, maybe he was afraid of losing her.

It pissed him off that one woman could alter him so much. But the fact that he was sure Rana was his soulmate smoothed his ruffled feathers.

***

Rana blamed Dallas for her sleepless nights. For the past several days, he'd been on the overnight shift at the firehouse. Her body was craving him. He'd spoiled her with his protective arms. Whenever they were around her, she drifted right off to sleep.

Considering the fact she'd be seeing Walton tomorrow for the first time in close to a year, made her groan. With all the BS she was sure he'd be shoveling, she needed all the rest she could get to deal with it.

She'd been tempted to invite Dallas with her to Charlotte, but thought that might have been too awkward for him. Having company on the two-hour drive certainly would have been nice. Too bad both her sisters were unavailable.

Her cell phone vibrated against the dresser, startling her. Lifting it, she smiled at Dallas's name. The smile grew wider when the picture of him filled her screen. Though it didn't show his face, she'd have known that body anywhere.

Instead of being naked—as she'd requested—he wore a white wife-beater tee, hiked to reveal his impressive six-pack and one pec. With his free hand, he had a thumb hooked inside his black boxers, pulling them low but not revealing much. She traced a finger over the screen, outlining that sexy V. It caused a tingle between her legs.

Another text came through.

I guess I am kinda that guy after all. But only for you. If you need a road-mate tomorrow, I'm free.

Rana's fingers eagerly responded.

You're my guy. And yes, I would love a road-mate. I'll see you at 10 am.

The following morning, Dallas insisted on driving to Charlotte. Rana protested several times, but, in the end, Dallas had gotten his way. But only because had they spent all morning going back and forth, they would have missed the service.

Dallas looked just as tempting in the black suit now as he had the night of Gadiya and Nico's wedding reception. So much had transpired since that night. Who could have guessed she would have ended up falling for that sexy fireman who kept flirting with her from across the room?

Every so often, Rana cut her eyes to Dallas. Though he hid it well, she could tell he was in need of rest. He'd downed an entire travel mug of coffee, kept massaging the side and back of his neck and yawning.

"Dallas, baby, you're exhausted."

He slid his gaze to her. "I'm good."

"Quit being so stubborn. Pull over and let me drive."

"Rana, baby, I'm fine," he said.

His tone was pacifying. Probably to get her to shut up and let him focus. Maybe he wasn't tired. Maybe there was something else going on with him. Could it have been the idea of coming face-to-face with Walton? No, she seriously doubted that one. Dallas was too confident to be intimidated.

When they arrived at the church, Rana and Dallas took a seat in the crowded sanctuary. One thing she could say about Ms. Hedda, she was loved and respected by many. Evident by the droves of people here to celebrate her homegoing.

Dallas captured her hand in his and brought it to his lips, kissing the back. "You okay?"

She'd shared with him how much she disliked funerals. Attending her mother's, brother's, and father's funerals had soured her on them because they brought back so much grief. Surprisingly, she was okay, and had a feeling he had something to do with it. Flashing a low-wattage smile, she said, "Yes."

After the service, everyone gathered in the church's large dining hall to eat, chat, and reminisce. Earlier, she'd locked eyes with Walton from across the room, but he never approached her, which had been just fine with her.

After speaking to several family members, Rana decided it was time to make their escape. Before they made it to the exit, Walton's sister, Tamra, grabbed Rana and pulled her into a warm embrace.

Tamra had always reminded Rana of Jill Scott. In looks and Tamra's ability to sing her ass off. When she'd bellowed "His Eye is on the Sparrow" earlier, it had left Rana in tears. Rana had gotten along well with all of Walton's family, especially his sisters who'd always welcomed her as part of their clan.

"Sis, I know you weren't leaving without saying hello to me," Tamra said.

"You were getting pulled in several different directions. I'd planned to call you tonight."

Tamra's eyes slid past Rana and settled on Dallas. "Hello. I'm Tamra. And you are…"

Dallas took Tamra's outstretched hand. "Dallas. I'm Rana's…" He cut his eyes to Rana, clearly not wanting to say something that would make her uncomfortable. "I'm sorry for your loss," he said, abandoning labeling himself.

"Dallas is my boyfriend," Rana said, filling in the blank for him.

"Oh. I see."

Tamra had always been the judgmental one out of the bunch; however, she could never find fault with her brother, always making excuses for his behavior. Rana could hear the judgment in her voice now, but she didn't care.

Tamra smiled. "Well, nice to meet you, Dallas." She shook his hand vigorously, then turned back to Rana. "Evelyn would be heartbroken if you left without saying hello. She's in the back. Just walk down that hall, it's the third door on the left. I'll keep your beau company."

Rana gave Dallas an are-you-okay-with-that look. When he nodded, she smiled and said, "I'll be right back."

"He's in good hands," Tamra said.

If you know what's good for you, you'll keep your hands to yourself. Walking away, Rana laughed at herself for sounding like a jealous lover.

Several moments later, she entered the room Tamra had directed her too. The junked-up space looked as if it hadn't been used for some time. Dusty chairs were stacked in one corner and rickety tables in another. "Evelyn, are you in here?"

"No, she's not."

Rana stilled, a cold chill crawling up her spine. Whipping around to face Walton, she leveled him with a razor-sharp gaze. At one point, the tall, almond-skinned man could cause butterflies in her stomach when those hazel eyes settled on her. Now, he simply caused her stomach to churn. "What are you doing here, Walton?" Clearly, she'd been set up.

"The question is, what are you doing at my mother's funeral with another man?"

"Another man? He's the *only* man." She just couldn't resist landing at least one jab. The power of petty.

Walton's jaw tightened, then released. "That's some disrespectful sh—" He paused as if remembering where they were.

"Ha. Kinda like screwing another woman in the bed we shared, huh?"

Walton sighed and washed a hand over his close-shaven head. "I'm hurting, Rana. I don't want to do this with you today. Not today."

"We're not going to do this at all, Walton. I'm

sorry for your loss, and you have my condolences." She started out of the room.

"I still love you, Rana. My mother was right. You were the best thing to had ever happened to me. I was too selfish to see it. Her dying wish was for me to make things right with you."

Rana's first thought went to Dallas, and she smiled. Comparing the man behind her to the one waiting out front for her was like pitting a sturdy foundation against a paper bridge. One you trusted to fully support you, while the other... Well, the other was utterly useless.

Turning, she said, "You have made things right with me, Walton. And for me. Your betrayal crushed me. And as a result, I closed myself off to all possibilities. Then someone came along and fought for the chance to get to know me. Fought tirelessly for what you freely gave away without so much as a blink of the eye."

"I made a mistake, Rana. I'm not perfect."

Rana laughed. "I never needed you to be. I just needed you to be true." She paused a moment, then tossed words at him she never imagined would have come out of her mouth. "I forgive you." It felt so rejuvenating, she repeated herself, "I forgive you. But I will never love you again. You don't deserve it...or me. Goodbye, Walton."

On the opposite side of the door, Rana took a moment to gather her thoughts. When she recalled what she'd just done, a full smile curled her lips. Something felt different. *She* felt different—lighter, freer. She felt...*closure*.

Returning to the vestibule, Rana spotted Dallas chatting with an older gentleman. Just like him to make friends wherever he went. When she approached, he flashed her one of those dazzling smiles that always seemed to make her day a little better.

"Hey," he said.

He took a moment to introduce her to his new friend, Jimmy Ander. The older gentleman's dark leathery face was etched with deep lines. The rough, calloused feel of his hands suggested he was no stranger to hard work. *Farmer's hands.* They reminded her of her grandfather's.

Jimmy Ander clapped Dallas on the shoulder. "Well, it was nice meeting the two of you. I'm going to get some of that fried chicken and potato salad 'fore it's all gone. Lord, that's one thing I'm sho' gon' miss 'bout Hedda. That woman sho' could cook." He shook his head and strolled away.

"Look at you making new friends," she teased once Jimmy Ander was gone.

"What can I say? People can't resist me."

"I won't dispute that." She wanted to kiss him, because she couldn't resist him either but felt it would have been inappropriate in their current setting. "What happened to Tamra? I thought she was supposed to be keeping you company."

"She got summoned way. To be honest, I couldn't have been happier."

Rana's brow furrowed. "Why, what

happened?" She knew Tamra could be a handful, but would she really cause friction at her own mother's funeral? Giving it a little thought, Rana answered, yes.

"Nothing really. Other than her telling me how happy you and her brother had once been, she was outstanding company."

Sarcasm dripped from his words.

"Oh, and she also told me how she prays every night that you two will get back together because that's what her mother wanted. Out of respect, I didn't remind her that some prayers go unanswered."

The same ole Tamra, always saying whatever foolishness swirled around in her head, regardless of the setting. "Pay her no mind. No one else does."

"Did everything go okay with your ex? That is who you were in the back with, wasn't it?"

Rana's lips parted, but nothing escaped. How could he possibly know she'd spoken to Walton?

"He strolled back into the room a short time after you did. Plus, the sister you were supposedly going to meet emerged from the kitchen a short time after you disappeared."

Supposedly. Disappeared. Why did it feel like he was accusing her of something? "I wasn't trying to sneak around or anything if that's what you're thinking."

He shrugged. "I'm not thinking anything, Rana. I just wanted to know if everything went okay, that's all."

"You're upset."

"Upset, no. Concerned, a little."

"Don't be. Today, I did something I didn't think I was capable of doing. I forgave him. You know why I forgave him? To free myself of the extra baggage I've been dragging around. Plus, ridding myself of it makes it a little easier for you to lift me."

Dallas's expression softened and his mouth curled into a half-smile. Hugging her to his chest, he said, "Let's get out of here."

"Okay."

He led her through the crowd.

"Are you two leaving?" came from behind them.

Rana flinched at the sound of Walton's voice. She eyed Dallas briefly before turning. "We are."

Walton's eyes left her and settled on Dallas. "I don't think we've met. Walton Childs."

Dallas accepted his outstretched hand. "Dallas Fontaine. Sorry for your loss."

"Thanks." Walton studied Dallas for a moment. "You have a good woman. Make sure you don't screw up."

A second later, he was gone.

"Wow. That was unexpected," said Rana.

"Yeah, but very good advice," Dallas said. "However, I imagine he's praying that I will. Unfortunately, it's one of those prayers that will never be answered."

Rana held Dallas's face between her hands. "You are my knight in shining armor, Dallas Fontaine."

9

Since he hadn't established a primary care physician in Mount Pleasance—something he really needed to do but had put off—Dallas reported to the medical center to have his annual exam performed. The deadline to have it completed was in two days, but of course, he'd waited until the last minute. That wasn't usually his M.O., but he hated doctors' offices.

Sitting in the drab room reminded him of just how much he hated them. It also reminded him of his father and the constant trips he'd made to the oncologist alongside the man.

Dallas clenched his jaw and tried not to dwell on the past. Instead, he eyed a framed picture of a lighthouse, hung on one of the sterile white walls. The room could have definitely used some color. *A yellow or green. Something cheery*. Since when did he start considering paint colors? He chuckled. *Since Rana*.

He scrutinized a vintage-style poster of North Carolina occupying another wall. Even the décor was dismal. His eyes rose to the generic black and white clock that hung over the door. Fifteen minutes had passed since he'd glanced at it last. Antsy, his leg shook from his increasing lack of patience.

What in the hell is taking so long?

As if he'd sent a cosmic wave through the building, there was a tap at the door. A beat later, the doctor entered. Mid-thirties, medium height and build with hair so blonde it glowed.

"Mr. Fontaine. I'm so sorry to keep you waiting. We're a bit behind schedule. Friday's can be a madhouse around here." He extended his hand. "Dr. Callahan."

Dallas took his hand and shook it firmly. "I was beginning to think you guys had forgotten about me."

"Not at all. Let's see if I can get you out of here ASAP." Dr. Callahan positioned the stool directly in front of Dallas, then eased onto it and scrolled through the tablet he'd entered with. "I see you're here for your fireman's exam."

Dallas nodded, wishing the man would do less talking and more examining so he could get out of there.

"Your vitals look great. No medical conditions. No allergies. I'll do a quick—but thorough—" he added, "physical exam. Any questions for me before we start?"

Dallas massaged the side of his face. "No, I don't think so."

"Okay, then. Let's get this show on the road."

When Dr. Callahan had said thorough, he hadn't lied. He checked Dallas' ears, nose, neck, skin, listened to his heart and lungs before moving below the waist. This part Dallas hated. The idea of anyone—other than Rana—fondling his junk didn't sit well with him.

Dr. Callahan examined his groin, penis, scrotum, then testicles. When he reached for a handheld light and placed it behind his right testicle, a hint of concern filled Dallas. Something was wrong. He could sense it.

Never pausing his inspection, Dr. Callahan said, "Do you perform testicular self-examinations?"

"Um, no." Concern set in deeper. "Is there something wrong, Doc?"

"Don't be alarmed, but I feel a...small, hard lump. About the size of a pea on the surface of your right testicle."

Don't be alarmed? Was he kidding? "A lump? Are you saying like...cancer?"

"I'm not saying anything yet, but I would like to do a few more tests. Blood work and an ultrasound. Depending on what they reveal, I may want to refer you to a specialist.

A specialist? Obviously, Dr. Callahan suspected something.

"Do you recall your last testicular examination by a physician?"

Dallas's head swam, and he had trouble processing the doctor's question. "Umm...last...last year? No, the year before last." He massaged his forehead and squeezed his lids together. "I can't..." The room grew scorching hot and his stomach churned. When Dr. Callahan patted him on the thigh, he flinched.

"Let's not worry about the date."

Dr. Callahan stood and informed Dallas he'd return shortly. Once the door clicked closed, Dallas sat forward and rested his elbows on his knees and steadied his breathing. He closed his eyes to subdue the spinning. *It's nothing*, he kept telling himself. *It's nothing*.

Cancer? No, the universe couldn't be this cruel. This couldn't be happening. Not now. Not when everything in his life was going right. Not when he'd finally found the one. An image of Rana flashed in his head. *It's nothing*.

That night, Dallas lay in bed next to Rana, his mind aching from Dr. Callahan's suspicion. Testicular cancer. He hadn't told Rana about the diagnosis and wouldn't. At least, not until he'd gotten a definitive diagnosis from his father's old oncologist in D.C. His mother had already made the appointment for first thing Monday morning.

There was no need to worry Rana at this point. He wanted to be a hundred percent sure of what he was dealing with. *Heck, it could be nothing at all, despite how sure Dr. Callahan had sounded. Hell, the man wasn't an oncologist. He could be wrong.*

Anger swelled inside Dallas, but Rana squirming in his arms doused his outrage. By the glow of the television, he watched her sleep in his arms. God, he desperately needed Dr. Callahan to be wrong.

As if she could feel him ogling her, Rana's eyes

fluttered open, and she smiled up at him. "Can't sleep?"

"Too much on my mind, I guess." *Damn. Wrong choice of words.*

Rana's brow furrowed. "Like what?"

Thinking quickly, he said, "This trip to DC on Monday. Dealing with Fontaine business matters always leads to a headache." As a cover, he'd told her he needed to make an impromptu visit home to sign some paperwork. He hated lying to her. But if he kept telling himself it was for the greater good, maybe he would eventually start to believe it. He'd sworn to her he'd always tell her the truth, but this had to be an exception.

Rana kissed his chin. "You sure you don't want me to come with you? For moral support."

She smiled, and his world got a little brighter. "If this weren't strictly a business trip, I would say yes, come with me. Actually, I would say hell, yes. But you and I both know I wouldn't make it out of the hotel if your warm, sexy body was stretched out next to me."

"Are you sure it's not because you're not ready for me to meet your family?"

"Do you really believe that?" Something sad flashed in Rana's eyes, and it broke his heart. He came up on his elbow and stared down at her. "Do you?"

She shrugged. "I don't know, Dallas, but I hope not."

"Woman, I love you. And I'd never hide you

from anyone. Especially my family. Trust me, they know all about you and have for a while."

Rana rose slowly, her eyes as wide as fifty cent pieces. Her mouth gaped open, but nothing came out.

The bewildered expression on her face troubled him. "What's wrong?"

"You... You just said... You just said you love you."

Damn, had he really allowed that to slip out? With so much on his mind... He grew silent for a moment, debating what to say next. He didn't want to scare her off, but he didn't want to keep hiding how he felt about her either. Especially now. "The night of Gadiya and Nico's wedding, I called my mother and told her I'd finally found you. That I'd finally found the one that makes my heart do flips." He dragged a finger along the side of her face. "There's nothing I wouldn't do for you, Rana Lassiter. Absolutely nothing. Including sacrificing my happiness for yours and shielding you from anything that could jeopardize your joy. That's how I know I love you."

Tears welled in her eyes. "I love you, too."

Dallas rested his forehead against hers and closed his eyes.

"Is everything okay?"

He forced a smile. "I'm perfect, baby. I'm perfect because I have you."

Rana cradled his face between her hands and studied him long and hard, clearly attempting to decide whether or not to believe him. Apparently, he'd been convincing enough, because a short time later, she kissed him gently on the lips before whispering, "Make love to me."

He wasn't sure if he was capable. Could he even get an erection knowing what was going on in that region of his body? The second Rana slid her hand down his boxers and gripped him, he swelled.

He wanted to push her away, tell her not tonight. But even despite the storm he was weathering, he couldn't deny himself the pleasure of making love to her.

"You feel ready to me," she said with a smirk.

Covering her mouth with his, Dallas kissed her hard and wild. Every drop of love, passion, and desire he felt for her seeped into the kiss. As hard as he tried, he couldn't get enough of her. Their moans intertwined and danced about the room.

His greedy kiss didn't halt when he positioned himself between her legs and entered her in one long, hard stroke. Rana's mouth broke away from his, and she cried out in what he hoped was satisfaction.

"Yes, Dallas!"

Giving her more of what she clearly wanted, he delivered one untamed stroke after another. The headboard banged against the wall, and he feared the picture of Rana hanging above his bed would come crashing down on them.

Dallas withdrew long enough to direct Rana onto all fours, then entered her again. He channeled every emotion he'd felt since leaving the medical center into his strokes, making love to her in a manner he hadn't before—completely uncontrolled, untamed and raw.

Rana moved her hips, meeting and welcoming each of his thrusts. On the brink of exploding, he held her firmly by the waist and delivered several more powerful strokes, then released a throaty sound that could have easily been mistaken for a ferocious beast.

Rana's cries mixed with his. A second later, she collapsed onto the bed, and he toppled over with her, still joined intimately. The orgasm was stronger than any other he'd experienced before. Rana pulsed around him, milking every drop of his seed.

"That was...intense," she said, through heavy breaths. "I loved every second of it."

Instead of responding, Dallas kissed the crook of her neck and her shoulder, then pulled her into his arms. "Let's sleep."

Rana responded with a moan and nestled ever closer to him. "You did it Dallas Fontaine, and I have no idea how."

"Did what?"

"Made me fall insanely in love with you. Something I was determined *not* to do."

At the words, Dallas's emotions spiked and nearly betrayed him. Pinching his lids together, he forced away the tears stinging his eyes. Actual tears. He couldn't remember the last time he'd cried. He hadn't at his grandmother's funeral, hadn't at his grandfather's, hadn't at his father's.

Getting himself together, he said, "Oh, you know how. This Fontaine charm is lethal." He hugged her just a little tighter. Several beats of silence had played before he spoke again, "Rana, baby, I have to tell you something."

Rana's head rose, and she stared down at him. "Okay. Tell me."

All he could do was gaze into her tender eyes. He wished this was all just a horrible dream he'd awaken from any minute now.

"Say something, Dallas. You're starting to scare me."

How did he say what he needed to say? How did he tell her he could be in for the fight of his life...literally? "I—" His words caught in his throat. Starting again, he said, "I...didn't use protection." Not exactly what he'd intended to say. But then, an even worse thought occurred to him. What if he'd gotten her pregnant? She'd be left the raise their child without him. What had he done?

Rana laughed, lowering her head back to his chest. "Calm down, lover boy. Don't worry. Your little soldiers aren't going to do any damage." Her head rose again. "Un...less you're trying to tell me your dick is a death rod."

This made Dallas laugh...hard. Only Rana could bring him joy at a time like this. He fixed his mouth to say he was as healthy as a horse, but that would have been a lie. Instead, he said, "You're safe with me, baby. You're always safe with me."

"Who knows, maybe one day I'll spit out a little one for you."

"Ten little ones. Nine boys and one girl," he joked.

"How about we meet somewhere in the middle? We have plenty of time to come to a compromise.

He prayed she was right.

***

Rana welcomed Sadona's unexpected visit to her shop. It wasn't like she was getting any work done anyway. She was too worried about Dallas. He'd sounded so exhausted when they'd spoken on the phone the night before. First thing this morning, she tried to call and check on him but hadn't been able to get him. And her last two calls had gone straight to voicemail.

Something was wrong. She could feel it.

She'd expected him back in town on Tuesday but had gotten a phone call from him Monday night saying it would be Wednesday before he returned. It was now Thursday and still no Dallas. Maybe the Fontaine business matter was more pressing than he'd let on.

Sadona's words broke into Rana's thoughts.

"I'm stealing you away from this place for a few hours. Tyrell can watch the store. We need a little retail therapy."

"I don't feel like shopping, Cutesy," Rana said, using the nickname their father had given Sadona.

Sadona arched a brow. "*You* don't feel like window shopping? Okay, who are you and what have you done with my sister? You know, the one who, at the mention of shopping, has her shoes on and is waiting at the front door."

"Do you remember that feeling I had right before mom, Phoenix, and dad died?"

Sadona's expression turned serious. "Yes. Why?"

Rana rested her hand on her quivering stomach. "I have that same feeling now. I haven't been able to get Dallas on the phone all morning. When I call, it goes straight to voicemail. I'm worried, Cutesy. Something is wrong. I can feel it."

Sadona's concerned expression turned tender. "You and I both know Dallas is not dying, Rana. Has anyone ever told you you're a worry wart?"

"Yes. Mainly you." Rana rolled her eyes away playfully. Inhaling deeply, then exhaling heavily, she said. "I just can't shake this feeling."

A slow smile curled Sadona's plum painted lips.

"What?" Rana said.

"You really love this man, don't you?"

Rana fell back against her leather office chair and sighed. "So much that the idea of anything happening to him scares the hell out of me. I'm not sure I'm equipped to handle emotions like these. I've never loved anyone so fervently. All I've done these past few days is worry about him. It was never like this with Walton. Never."

Sadona's expression turned sad. "That's the one thing I miss the most. Having someone to worry about and to worry about me."

Rana reached across the desk and took Sadona's hand into hers. "You'll always have Gadiya and me to worry about. And we'll worry about you, too."

Something dawned on Rana. Sadona didn't like to shop...ever. That was Rana and Gadiya's thing. Rana had been so lost in her own forged turmoil, she hadn't recognized Sadona's. Sadona was lonely.

Changing her tone, Rana said, "You know what?" she came from behind the desk and stood next to a seated Sadona. "On second thought, I could use a little retail therapy."

"Great!" Sadona stood. "And afterward, if you're still worried about Dallas, we'll just keep on driving 'til we reach Washington. How hard could it be to locate the Fontaines of DC?"

They shared a bout of much-needed laughter.

Rana draped her arms around her sister. "You're the best big sister any girl could have. But you're right. I'm just being a worry wart. I'm sure everything is fine." She brushed the eerie feeling aside and hooked her arm through Sadona's. "Let's go shopping."

10

Dallas sat directly across from his father's old oncologist, Dr. Newell, in the man's modestly decorated office, along with his mother and Denver. It hadn't surprised him that his mother had handled his testicular cancer diagnosis so well. Denver, on the other hand... Dallas slid a glance in Denver's direction. If his brother's leg bounced any faster and harder, every book on Dr. Newell's case would tumble to the floor.

Instead of Dallas focusing on Dr. Newell as he rattled on about the ultrasound he'd taken on Monday, the additional blood tests he'd taken Tuesday and Wednesday, the blood tumor marker tests, and acronyms like AFPs and HCGs, he was focused on the numerous awards affixed to the wall behind the man.

By all accounts, Dr. Newell was the very best in his field. That fact alone should have given Dallas some consolation. It hadn't. In his mind, cancer was cancer and equated to a death sentence. What had he done to deserve this?

An image of Rana filled his thoughts. This time, thinking about her didn't fill him with the usual euphoria he experienced when she occupied his head. It flooded him with sadness and despair. How would she react when he told her?

"After your radical inguinal orchiectomy, the

operation to remove the tumor, testicle and spermatic cord," he explained, "we'll start you on a course of chemo—"

"Will I be sterile, doc?" Of all the questions he could have asked, this one seemed most important at the moment. His eyes met Dr. Newell's again. The man reminded him of that television doctor that played the chief on that medical series. What was it? Something anatomy? Same chocolate skin, same salt and pepper hair. Same commanding presence. What was the name of that show? Dallas abandoned trying to figure it out. It didn't matter. This wasn't some damn scripted show; this was real life. His life.

Dr. Newell rolled his pen between his fingers—an expensive looking instrument he'd probably paid a fortune for. Dallas couldn't help but wonder how many times he'd used it to scribe the word cancer.

Cancer. Was this a family curse? His great-grandfather. His grandfather. His father. All different types, but still the same ole dirty bastard. *Cancer*.

"That is a possibility, Dallas. However—"

Dallas didn't wait for Dr. Newell to complete his thought. He rushed to his feet, walked over to the floor to ceiling window, and stared out at the bustling city below. Denver came to stand beside him and wrapped his arm around his shoulders. He appreciated his brother not attempting to comfort him with well-intended, but useless-at-the-moment, words.

Dr. Newell continued, "—as a precaution, you can store sperm in a sperm bank. In vitro fertilization is a viable option."

Dallas folded his arms across his chest. Dr. Newell continued to talk about being able to stage his cancer once he received the pathologist's report after the surgery on Friday, and how there would be additional tests to see if cancer had metastasized to other parts of the body. X-rays, CT scans, MRI scans, PET scans.

So many damn acronyms.

Based on the blood work results, Dr. Newell made an educated guess it was stage II and was confident Dallas would make a full recovery.

Dallas closed his eyes and drifted away as his mother ticked off her list of questions. *Ten. Nine boys and one girl.* He laughed to himself remembering the conversation he and Rana had had about children.

"I'm with you, bro. All the way. We're going to beat this. We're in this together."

Denver's voice cracked, and Dallas knew the man was struggling to hold back his emotions. He gave Denver a fist bump, then set his sights back out the window. Dallas washed a hand over his mouth. If he couldn't give Rana babies, what good would he be in her life? Was it even fair for him to burden her with this?

He recalled his words to Rana the night he'd confessed his love. *There's nothing I wouldn't do for you, Rana Lassiter. Absolutely nothing. Including sacrificing my happiness for yours and shielding you from anything that could jeopardize your joy. I love you that much.*

Despite how much the idea hurt him, he knew what had to be done.

***

Rana all but leaped from the couch to retrieve her cell phone sitting on a table by her front door. "It's Dallas," she said to Sadona, a wave of relief washing over her. Swiping her thumb across the screen, she didn't waste a precious second greeting him. "I've been calling you all day. Are you okay? I've been worried senseless."

"Rana—"

Pacing back and forth, she continued, cutting Dallas off mid-thought. "I've had this eerie feeling all day—actually since you left on Monday—that something is wrong."

"Rana—"

"And when I couldn't reach you *all day*," she emphasized, "I—"

"Rana, stop!"

The volume and sternness in Dallas's voice paused her steps and rambling. It also brought Sadona to the edge of the couch, her face contorting. Apparently, she'd heard Dallas, too.

Rana pulled the phone from her ear and eyed the screen curiously, making sure it was actually

Dallas's name there. He'd never raised his voice to her before. Placing the phone back to her ear, she said, "What is wrong with you?"

"I need you to not talk and just listen."

The man on the opposite end of the line sounded so foreign to her, it was baffling. "Okay, I'm listening."

A beat of silence played over the line, followed by a heavy sigh from Dallas. She hugged one arm around her waist and started to pace again. What was Dallas trying to build up to say? Based on their interaction thus far, whatever it was, wasn't good.

"I'm listening, Dallas," she repeated, hoping it would prompt him.

"I..." Another pause lingered. "I thought I was ready, Rana. I truly did. But...I'm not."

Rana shook her head, releasing a nervous laugh. "I don't understand. You're not ready? Not ready for what?"

"Us," he said plainly.

Rana stopped as if a wall had just fallen from the sky into her path. The air seized in her lungs and she struggled to snatch in a breath. "W-what?"

Dallas continued in a firm, emotionless tone, "I should have ended things a while ago. Before they'd gotten this far, but..." His words trailed.

Rana placed a trembling hand on her forehead, her head spinning from a mix of confusion and mounting anger. Releasing a humorless laugh, she said, "Before they'd gotten this far?"

"I thought I could learn to..."

Whatever he'd intended to say faded. A second later it sounded as if he'd placed a hand over the mouthpiece. When his voice traveled over the line again, his tone mirrored his previous one.

"I tried to make this something it wasn't. Something it's not. Something it can never be. You were right. You don't fit into my world, Rana. I'm sorry. I have to go."

"You have to go?" Rana slapped a tear from her cheek. "You have to go?" she repeated, disgust now dripping from her words. "You call to break up with me over the phone, and you have to go? You coward. You...coward," she said through tears. "You make me fall in love with you, then—" The painful lump of emotion in her throat trapped the remainder of her words. Lowering onto the arm of the loveseat, she said, "How, Dallas? How could you do this to me? You told me you loved me. You told me you loved me."

Dallas didn't utter one word. Had it not been for the faint rustling, she would have thought he'd disconnected.

A few more seconds had passed before he spoke again. "I hope someday you'll be able to forgive me."

The line went dead.

The cell phone dropped from her shaking hand and hit the floor with a thud. Sadona crossed the floor and knelt at her side. This had to be a nightmare. Dallas loved her and she loved him. This had to be a nightmare, one that she desperately wanted to wake from.

***

Dallas hurled his cell phone across the room, causing it to smash against the wall and separate into two pieces. Ignoring Denver, who'd been present during his phone call with Rana, he leaned forward and rested his elbows on his knees and attempted to recover from the conversation.

Damn, he hated himself so much right now. He'd hurt the one woman who he loved more than life itself. But forcing her to suffer through what was to come would hurt her more. He'd witnessed the toll this dreaded disease had taken on his mother as his father slowly deteriorated. No way could he do that to Rana.

Sure, Dr. Newell had said his chances of survival were good, but how could the man be certain? How could he give Rana that hope and risk it being snatched away, because Dr. Newell *said so*? No, he'd made the right decision. But it hurt. It hurt like hell.

"It had to be done," Dallas said.

From the second he'd shared his plan with his brother, Denver had disapproved. Even now, Dallas could sense Denver's objection. But it was done now. He'd freed Rana. He blocked out the memory of her cracking voice and sniffling. She would hate him for a lifetime, but he would love her for his—for as long as he had left.

Coming to his feet, Dallas walked through the French doors and onto the balcony. He stared out at the hundreds of acres that made up Fontaine Estates. In the past, the view gave him endless joy. Now, it all seemed...mundane.

None of it impressed him as it had before. Not the dozens of pristinely manicured topiary trees. Not the many finely trimmed bushes. Not the hundreds of flowering petals. None of it. Not even the sparkling pond in the distance he'd foolishly envisioned proposing to Rana by.

Life had dealt him one shitty hand.

The warm breeze that brushed across his face reminded him of the sensations he experienced from Rana's delicate touch, experienced each time they kissed, each time they made love. He braced himself against the stone banister and hung his head in despair. All of his dreams of spending a lifetime with her, shattered.

By nature, he'd never been a whining man, but this wasn't fair. It wasn't fucking fair.

"Why does it feel like you're giving up before you've even begun to fight," came from Denver, still standing inside the room.

A second later, the bedroom door opened, then slammed closed.

The magnitude of it all—the diagnosis, losing Rana, his brother's words—overwhelmed him. The wall he'd erected to shield him from exposing emotions crumbled like drywall, allowing in a myriad of feelings. Too many to contain.

Dallas gripped the stone with so much force, his fingers burned. Pinned up rage, fear, disbelief, regret caused an ache in his chest. Moments later, a deafening, tormented scream blasted past his lips.

11

All Rana wanted to do was forget she'd ever met Dallas Fontaine. Forget she'd ever fallen in love with him. Forget how he'd left a hole in her heart the size of Texas. Forget how he'd left her scarred. Forget how he'd left her all alone.

How could she still love the man who hadn't had the decency to dump her face-to-face? *Because you're a fool, Rana Lassiter. Just let him go.* But she couldn't because she didn't know how. Dallas had touched her in a way no man had ever come close to doing.

How could she have been so blind? Why hadn't she seen this coming? None of it made sense. What was wrong with her? Why did she always attract the wrong man? A myriad of chaotic emotions thundered inside of her, but she refused to shed one more tear for Dallas Fontaine.

"Okay, who wants daiquiris?" Gadiya said, joining Rana and Sadona in Rana's living room.

"None for me," Rana said, hugging her legs to her chest.

"I can make you a sangria or—"

Rana held up her hand. "I'm fine, Gadi." She rested her hand on her stomach. "I think those hot wings are fighting back."

"I guess so. You ate like fifty of them," Sadona said.

Gadiya and Sadona laughed, and Rana managed a chuckle.

Rana tossed a pillow at Sadona. "I'm an emotional eater. That or the fact I might be a little pregnant."

The laughter ceased instantly. Gadiya and Sadona stared at her wide-eyed and jaw-dropped, speechless.

This wasn't exactly how she'd planned to spring the news on her sisters that she might be carrying Dallas's child. She'd actually wanted to take one of the fifteen pregnancy tests she'd purchased the day before when her cycle was officially a week and a half late, but she'd been too afraid to do it alone. She needed her sisters.

As expected, Sadona was the first to recover from the shock of Rana's words. "Pregnant?"

Gadiya squealed. "I'm going to be an auntie. I hope it's twins. Mommy used to say twins run in the family."

Rana released an exasperated sigh. "I'm not having twins, Gadi. I don't even know for sure that I'm pregnant." She shrugged. "But my sore breasts and missed period would suggest I could be."

"I'll run to the pharmacy and grab a test," Gadiya said, halfway to the front door.

"No need. I have several. I've just been too afraid to take one." Sadona rubbed Rana's knee, the simple act calming her shaky nerves.

"Come on," Sadona said, taking her hand and directing her off the couch. "No use sitting around wondering."

Sadona led the way toward the bathroom. Rana stopped, reality hitting her like a grenade. "Oh, God. What if...? I can't—"

"Let's not worry until we know for sure," Sadona said, her tone soothing.

Rana nodded. "You're right. It's probably just stress." Yep, that was it. Stress.

A half hour later, they all stared at the line of positive pregnancy tests on the counter.

Rana rubbed her collarbone vigorously. "Maybe I should take—"

Gadiya cut Rana off mid-thought. "I'm pretty sure ten positive tests mean you're having a baby."

Rana ignored the excitement she heard in her sister's tone and dropped down onto the closed toilet seat lid. She buried her face in her hands. "*Shit, shit, shit*. How did this happen?" Rana jabbed a finger at Gadiya. "Don't answer that." Knowing her sister would give her a birds and the bees type explanation.

She and Dallas had only had unprotected sex once. Plus, she was on the pill.

Sadona, the voice of reason, spoke, "You have to tell Dallas, Rana. No matter how you feel about him, he deserves to know he's going to be a father."

Rana nodded. "I will."

She'd stick a note on his door. He'd eventually have to return to Mount Pleasance to clear out his house. She'd show him the same courtesy he'd shown her.

***

Dallas tightened the hand-stitched quilt around his body. One of the side effects from his chemo treatments was that he was always cold. And tired. And sick to his stomach. *And, and, and*. The list went on. Honestly, he wasn't sure how much more he could take. And he had three more months of this misery?

A tap sounded on his bedroom door. "Come in." A beat later, Harmen strolled in.

Harmen was considered a permanent fixture in the Fontaine household. The man had worked for—or with, as his father had always stated—their family since well before Dallas was born. They all considered him family.

In his early sixties, Harmen showed no signs of slowing down. Which was a good thing because Dallas didn't like the idea of the man not being around.

"Squeaky, you all right in here? Been cooped up in this room all day long."

Even though he was a grown man, Harmen still called Dallas by the nickname he'd given him as a child because he'd loved sneaking into places he wasn't supposed to be in. Harmen had said he was like a little squeaky mouse.

Without prompting, Harmen moved to the curtains and opened them wide. Dallas shielded his eyes from the sunlight that poured in, then protested as if the rays would cause him to spontaneously combust.

"Shut those!" His tone was hoarse, and his throat burned when he spoke, probably because he hadn't said much to anyone these past few weeks.

Harmen ignored him and opened the curtains even wider. "Mrs. is worried about you. Tells me you seem determined to wither away in this bedroom alone. I assured her I won't allow that to happen. Not on my watch."

Dallas pulled one of the goose-down pillows over his head to block out the light and Harmen's intrusion. "I'm fine."

"*Mmm-hmm.*"

When Harmen's lips smacked, Dallas knew the man was sucking on the old-fashioned horehound candy he liked so much.

"Does this *fine* have anything to do with the young lady you set free back in Mount Pleasance? Squabble told me everything."

Denver had earned the named Squabble because he had been notorious for getting into fights on the playground over the most trivial things.

Dallas wasn't surprised Denver had confided in Harmen. For as long as he could recall, they'd both been able to talk to him about anything. Though this time, Dallas wished Denver had kept his mouth shut.

When a chair creaked, Dallas knew Harmen

had settled into it, which meant this wasn't going to simply be a fly-by visit. Harmen remained quiet, and Dallas understood why. *Always look a man in the eyes. It's a show of respect,* Harmen had constantly reminded them.

Giving Harmen the respect he deserved, Dallas used what energy he had to prop himself against the headboard. He locked onto Harmen's dark brown gaze. "Go ahead. Let me have it."

Harmen laughed a jolly sound. "Let you have what?"

"The speech. Tell me how I'm a fool for letting Rana go. The only woman I've ever loved more than life itself. The only woman who has ever made me want to settle down, start a family. The only woman I've ever sacrificed my own happiness for." Dallas pounded a fist against his palm. "Tell me how I should have given her the opportunity to decide for herself whether or not she wanted to deal with...this." He fanned his hand over his much thinner body. "You saw me after my first chemo treatment, Harmen. Now you tell me, would any woman stay around for months of that? Hmm? The vomiting. Diarrhea. Shakes." His voice cracked. "I don't want her to see me like this. Half a damn man."

"Mmm-hmm." Harmen swished the candy around in his mouth. "Do you love this woman?"

Dallas's brow furrowed. Of all people, Harmen knew the answer to the question. Dallas had talked at length with the man about the woman who'd stolen every inch of his heart. "You know I do."

Harmen scrutinized him. "Do you really love her?"

"Yes. Why do you—?"

"Does she love you?" Harmen asked, cutting Dallas off mid-sentence. "And tell me what you know, not what you think."

In his head, Dallas replayed damn near every moment he'd spent with Rana. "Yes."

Harmen burst into laughter. "That's a good feeling, ain't it? To know a woman loves you." He stood and moseyed toward the door.

Confused, Dallas said, "Where are you going?"

"To watch reality TV. I much prefer to watch those crazy folks fight each other than to watch you fight against yourself."

"What does that mean?"

"It means that I don't think this is about that young lady at all. It's about you and your own vanity. *You* don't want her to see you like this. *You* think you're half a man. Out your own damn mouth, you said that woman loves you. And for you to know that she had to have not only told you, but shown you. *Half a man*." Harmen scoffed. "I bet you're still a whole man to her because, when you love someone, truly love them, their shell doesn't matter." He placed his hand over his heart. "Only this matters. Only this matters," he repeated, then left the room.

Before Dallas could consider Harmen's words, his cell phone rang. Nico's name flashed across the screen. Getting his thoughts together, he took the call. “What’s up, man?”

“Hey. Had you on my mind. How you doing, bro? You need anything?”

Apparently, Nico had him on his mind every day around this time. “I’m maintaining.” Nico was the only one in Mount Pleasance—other than the doctor at the medical center—who knew about his condition. He trusted Nico with the information, but had made him swear not to breathe a word of it to his wife. “What’s up in Mount Pleasance?”

“Um...same ole, same ole.”

Though Dallas never directly mentioned Rana’s name, he knew that Nico knew what he was actually asking was how Rana was. Nico always answered the same way: everybody’s good. But not today, and it troubled Dallas.

“Nico, man, is everybody good?”

“Yeah, yeah. The important question is how are you?”

Dallas swung his legs over the side of the bed and sat on the edge. He knew Nico well enough to know something was wrong. But what? And why was Nico being so damn elusive?

“Is she okay?” Dallas finally said. When Nico sighed, a bad feeling washed over Dallas. “What’s wrong, Nico?”

“Nothing. Nothing, man. Everyone and everything is good.”

Dallas wasn’t wholly convinced. But what could he do, short of going to Mount Pleasance to see for himself? That was not an option. However, he could have Denver snoop around since he was on his way there to retrieve the painting of Rana.

He shook off the idea. It wasn't fair to ask Denver to do that. He would just have to take Nico's word that all was good, despite his gut telling him otherwise.

12

On her way home from her OB appointment, Rana decided to swing by Dallas's place and finally leave the baby notification she'd ridden around with for the past several weeks. Sadona and Gadiya had both urged her to call him and have a civilized conversation. But since she wasn't feeling too refined these days when it came to Dallas Fontaine, she chose to do it her way. Regardless of how childish and petty it was.

Making a left onto Dallas's street, Rana stopped in the middle of the road when she spotted Dallas's SUV in the driveway. A flicker of excitement ignited in the part of her that had obviously forgotten she hated him. Stomping it down to nothing more than a memory, she weighed her options. Confront him like an adult or flee like a child.

She opted for the former. She was about to be a mother. Every decision she made from now on had to be in the best interest of her unborn child. And that meant telling Dallas face-to-face that during their heated night of passion they'd conceived a child.

Rana rested her hand on her stomach. "I'll always do what's best for you. I promise." Taking a deep breath, she eyed the house. "You can do this, Rana."

Parking by the curb, she took another deep breath, released it, and exited her vehicle. By the time she reached the front door, several beads of sweat ran down the back of her neck. She didn't know whether to blame the brutal summer heat or hormones for the fact she felt as if she were the main dish at a pig roast.

Noticing the door ajar, she entered. The second she stepped inside, a rush of memories flooded her like a breached levy. Painful and raw emotions swirled inside her. *Hold it together.*

A loud thud overhead caused her to jerk. Instinctively, her hand shielded her stomach. A mother's protective nature, she reasoned. Climbing the stairs, she headed toward the sound of the commotion. Dallas's bedroom.

When she pushed the door open, she froze. A man stood on the bed, removing the picture of her from the wall. He had a similar build as Dallas and the same smooth chocolate skin tone. It had to be his brother Denver. "Hello," she said.

Denver shuttered and nearly toppled off the edge of the bed.

He regained his balance. "You scared the..." Allowing his words to trail, he hopped down.

For a second or two, all she could do was stare at Denver, seeing Dallas all in him. "Umm, I'm Rana. Rana Lassiter."

"I know who you are," he said, offering his hand. "Denver Fontaine. Dallas's brother."

She smiled, taking his hand. "I know." Denver

was an inch or two shorter than Dallas, but there was no denying their kinship.

"I was actually looking for Dallas. Is he here?"

Something sad flashed in Denver's eyes. "No, he's not."

Denver's lips parted as if he wanted to say more but obviously reconsidered.

Her eyes slid to the picture now propped against the headboard, then back to Denver. "I see."

Awkward silence played between them.

Rana dug into her purse and removed the envelope. "Do you mind giving him this for me?"

Curiosity played on Denver's face as he took the parcel she offered. "Sure," he said, sliding it into his back pocket.

"Thanks. It was nice meeting you, Denver."

"Same here."

Rana smiled, then started out of the room.

"He needs you, Rana."

Rana faced Denver again, prepared to tell him just how unneeded his brother had made her feel. But something about the expression on Denver's face told her something wasn't right. "What is it?"

Denver's jaw flexed several times. Was he debating whether or not to tell her? No way was he getting away without telling her what was going on.

"What is it, Denver?" Her tone was harsher than she'd intended. Pressing her hand to her stomach and softening her tone, she said, "Please."

"Dallas—" Denver's words hitched and his gaze floated away. Bringing it back, he said, "Dallas has cancer. Testicular."

Rana watched Denver's lips continue to move, but she didn't process anything after the word cancer. It bounced around in her head like one of those metal balls in a pinball machine. Had he really just said what she thought he'd said? That Dallas had cancer. The air in the room grew thick, and bile burned the back of her throat. *Cancer. Dallas has cancer.* She swayed, her head spinning.

Denver's hands rose as if to catch her. "Are you okay?"

"I need...to sit down."

Denver took her arm and led her to the bed. Easing down, she focused on catching her breath.

"I'll get you some water."

Rana shook her head. "I'm fine." It was a pure lie. She was far from fine. "I need to see him, Denver." She rushed to her feet but dropped back to the bed when the room seemed to be shifting on its side.

"Just relax a minute," Denver said, kneeling next to her. "Dallas would kill me if anything happened to you."

Rana's eyes clouded with tears. It all made sense now. Dallas had pushed her way because he was sick and didn't want to burden her. "Will you take me to him?" She swiped a hand across her cheek. "I have to see him." Regardless of what Denver said, in several hours, she would be in D.C.

Even if she had to drive herself.

Denver flashed a pained expression, then nodded.

"Thank you."

"You do know he's going to kill me, right? For telling you, and especially for bringing you back with me." He came to his full height. "But hey, the real thing has to be better than a painting."

Rana's brow furrowed. "He sent you here for the painting?"

Denver nodded again. "I'm going to put it in the SUV. Take your time." He disappeared through the door.

Rana attempted the mindful breathing technique Gadiya had taught her, but her brain was too stimulated to concentrate. Taking several more minutes to get herself together, she joined Denver.

The drive to D.C. was relatively quiet. Mainly because she'd kept her face planted in her cell phone screen reading everything she could find on testicular cancer. She wanted to know what they were dealing with.

According to numerous sources, Dallas had an excellent chance of survival. That filled her with so much joy a tear trickled down her cheek. When she wiped it away, she could feel Denver's eyes on her. Probably trying to access whether or not she was on the verge of having some sort of breakdown.

"Are you okay?" he finally asked.

"Yes, I'm fine," she said, eyeing him. "Should I bring your mother flowers?" She realized how silly the question was the second it had left her lips.

Denver laughed. "My mother?"

Rana chuckled at the comical expression on his face, then brushed the words off. "Never mind."

Dallas had told her their mother loved fresh flowers and orchids. Since she was barging into the woman's home, Rana thought flowers would have been a good touch. But truthfully, Mrs. Fontaine's acceptance was the least of her concerns.

***

Dallas relaxed on the covered patio with his mother, watching the sun set. The scent of fragrant flowers swirled around them, and the sound of bees buzzed in the air. The reds, oranges, and yellows of the horizon meshed into a continuous burst of colors. It was nice.

She scene reminded him of his time with Rana in the meadow some time back. He chuckled recalling how she yelped, gasped, and *wup-wup-wup* as he attempted to teach her how to ride his motorcycle.

"Are you okay, son?"

No, he wasn't but smiled and nodded for his mother's benefit. Why couldn't he stop thinking about Rana? Why couldn't he simply forget her, the way he'd done so many other women from his past. *Because she wasn't like any other woman from my past*. Regardless, he had to forget her or drive himself insane. Forget their life together.

Forget how she made him feel. Forget how much he had loved her. *Still* loved her.

"It's nice. The breeze," his mother said.

His mother's words freed him from the dark abyss of memories. Although he was wrapped up like a burrito, the soft gust of air did feel good across his face. "Yes, it is."

"Are you comfortable? Can I get you anything?"

A new ball, a clean bill of health, and Rana. "I'm fine." Even if he weren't he wouldn't have told her. His mother worried too much. The stress was taking its toll on her. Those usually bright eyes had lost some of their glow. Dallas knew it was because of him and hated that fact. But as usual, June Fontaine wore a radiant front of strength.

Her warm, delicate hand rested on his covered arm. "How do you feel?"

Surprisingly, he felt better today than he had in a long while. Maybe it was the fact that tonight he'd fall asleep staring at Rana's image on his wall. "I feel great." Whether or not she believed him, he didn't know, but she smiled.

"Wonderful. Just let me know if that changes."

Another stretch of silence played between them. Dallas closed his eyes but popped them open when an image of Rana materialized. The memories of Rana would kill him before cancer could. "I love you, Mom. Thank you for everything you do for me, everything you've done. I haven't said that enough. Thank you."

"You're my son, Dallas. There's nothing in this world I wouldn't do for you or your brother. I'd trade places with you right now if I could. This very instance."

"Don't say that. The thought of you going through this..." He shook his head. "Please don't say that."

"God's going to send you a miracle, son. A beautiful miracle."

Dallas parted his lips to speak, but Denver's entrance made him pause.

"Hey, folks," Denver said.

Dallas didn't bother turning. "Hey."

"Hi, dear," his mother said, turning. "Oh. Hello."

"Hello."

The familiar voice froze Dallas solid. *Couldn't be*. He had to be hallucinating. Loosening the quilt so he could move, he turned. *Rana?* A euphoric sensation rushed through his entire body. He hadn't been tired before, but her presence exhausted him. He fought the desire to rush to her and envelope her in his arms.

It had felt like an eternity since he'd seen her last. She was gorgeous, far more breathtaking than he remembered. And she glowed. In the midst of appreciating Rana's presence, reality kicked in, turning his appreciation to anger. She couldn't see him like this.

He sent a narrow-eyed, heated gaze in Denver's direction. "Why did you bring her here?"

"I—"

Before Denver could finish his thought, Rana cut in. "He didn't have a choice."

"You shouldn't have come," Dallas said, turning a stern eye to Rana. His tone was brutal, and he regretted every second of the frigidness he gave off, but he had to be convincing, had to encourage her to want nothing to do with him. But each word he spoke broke his heart.

Rana blatantly ignored him as if he hadn't spoken a single syllable. She slid her gaze away, placing him on hold, and neared his mother.

Rana offered her hand. "It's a pleasure to meet you, Mrs. Fontaine. I've heard a lot about you. I'm Rana. Rana Lassiter. I apologize for barging into your home unannounced. And a beautiful home you have."

When his mother flashed a warm, welcoming smile, Dallas knew Rana had won the woman over. *Less than five minutes*. Rana had set a record.

"No apology necessary. It's nice to finally meet you, dear. I've heard a lot about you, too."

Rana eyed Dallas briefly. "All good things I hope."

Nothing but good, he wanted to say. When his mother had asked why Rana wasn't there by his side, he'd told her everything. And though she'd remained silent on the matter, he'd witnessed a similar look of disappointment on her soft brown face as he had on Denver's.

Well, his mother seemed pretty damn

talkative now. As his mother offered Rana tea and a meal after "what had to be an exhausting ride," she'd said, Dallas fixed a hard stare of disapproval on his brother. Denver had never betrayed him this way before.

Denver's jaw clenched as if there was something he wanted to say but battled to keep it to himself. His silence irritated Dallas even more. Why did everyone believe he was so damn fragile?

Instead of stating whatever was on his mind, Denver backed away and escaped inside. Dallas refocused on Rana and his mother. The fact that they appeared to be getting along so well would have made him extremely happy, had the circumstances been different. But they weren't.

"Mom, may I speak with Rana privately?"

A concerned expression danced on his mother's face. For a brief moment, he thought she would actually say no.

"Sure, son." Turning back to Rana, she said, "It was a pleasure meeting you."

"You as well," Rana said.

His eyes never left Rana as his mother ambled away. It was all he could do to keep from snatching her into his arms and telling her how much he'd missed her, how much he loved her. But he couldn't. Dammit, he couldn't. "Go home, Rana. I don't want you here."

"Instead, you'd prefer to have a painting of me?"

Apparently, she knew why he'd sent Denver to

North Carolina. He released a humorless laugh, hating himself even more for what he was about to say. "Why can't you take a damn hint? I don't want you."

By the solemn expression on her face, he'd done what he'd set out to do, make her want to leave. She wasn't the only casualty of his words. So was he. By breaking her, he was snuffing out whatever light still managed to flicker inside him. After today, he'd never be the same again.

Then the strangest thing happened. Rana smiled at him. Was she about to snap?

"I never told you how my father died, Dallas. Stage four liver cancer."

The revelation surprised him, but it didn't change anything.

"Just like you, he was determined to push everyone away. Especially the ones who loved him the most. He begged to be placed in an assisted living facility to die alone. I thought his behavior was the cruelest, most selfish act I'd ever experienced. We loved him. Why in the world would he want to push us away?"

Rana's eyes glistened, but no tears feel. He prayed none would.

"Sadona helped Gadiya and me understand that what our father was doing, in his mind, was an act of pure love. He didn't want to burden us. Didn't want us to see him vulnerable. Wanted to spare us the pain of watching him die."

Tears streamed down her face, and Dallas

wanted desperately to wipe them away. But if he touched her soft skin, his defenses would shatter. He had to stay strong.

Rana continued, "What he didn't get was that, despite his good intentions, he was robbing us. Robbing us of precious moments we could have spent loving him. I get it. I get that our father thought he was protecting us. But he wasn't. He was crushing us. All we wanted, the only thing we wanted, was to love him for as long as he had left."

For a brief second, he considered whether he was making a mistake by pushing her away. But the second he recalled the fact that there was a possibility he could never give her children, that chemo may not leave him cancer-free, that he couldn't even get a damn erection, he knew he was doing the right thing.

Turning his back to her, he said, "Dammit, Rana. Just go."

Rana's tone turned to stone. "You don't know me, Dallas Fontaine. Not like you should. If you did, you would have known that I would have stood right by your side every step of this journey. I'm a Lassiter woman. Lassiter women stand by their men. Through good, through bad, through everything in between. I'm a Lassiter woman, and I plan to stand by you. My man."

When she paused, Dallas assumed she'd walked away. But a second later she spoke again, her tone much softer this time.

"I love you, Dallas Fontaine. I love you. And I

want to be here for you. But you have to want me here. You have to want me on this journey with you. And if you're pushing me away because you think I can't handle this, you're dead wrong."

Dallas whipped around, her words triggering something in him. "Dead is exactly what I might be, Rana. I have stage two testicular cancer that has spread to nearby lymph nodes."

Rana started rattling off facts about testicular cancer like she'd been nominated the poster-child for the disease. How the disease was highly responsive to chemotherapy, how the survival rate was over ninety percent.

"I didn't hear you mention anything about erectile dysfunction," he said. "I can't get it up, Rana. Your sexual appetite is as grand as mine. What happens when I can't please you?"

Rana shook her head slowly. "Dallas, what we share is much deeper than sex. Do you think there has to be penetration for you to please me?"

"Yes!"

"Baby, when we're intimate, it's not your sticking your dick inside me that arouses me. It's everything that comes before that point. The way you kiss me—slow and gentle, fast and hard. The way your hands and mouth explore my body—patiently, inquisitively. The way you whisper in my ear, telling me all the things I long to hear. The way you cherish me, Dallas, is true pleasure. And you give it so well."

Steadfast and determined. Did he think he

ever stood a chance against this woman? "I'm not the man you fell in love with." He'd lost weight, the muscles that once caused a sparkle in her eyes were gone. "My body—"

"Is as beautiful as it has always been. Your shell is not what I fell in love with, Dallas. I fell in love with that confident, persistent, and sometimes nuisance-of-a-man who was *determined* to have me. I fell in love with the man who I had no other choice but to fall in love with." She blinked rapidly. "I fell in love with the man...with the man I want to love for eternity."

Dallas scrubbed his hand over his lips several times. He turned away again and pinched the bridge of his nose as if the move would cause the tears burning his eyes to evaporate. "Rana, what if—" He swallowed the painful lump of emotion in his throat. "What if I told you there's a chance I'll never be able to give you children?"

Rana moved around and stood in front of him, wiping the moisture from his cheeks. "I would say there's absolutely no way that can be true."

"Are you predicting the future now?"

"Not everyone's. Just ours."

Their future. It was a beautiful concept. Dallas rested a hand on her neck, then brushed his thumb over her jawline. "I guess there's no getting rid of you, huh?"

"Do you really want to?"

"I never wanted to. You'll never fully understand how much I love you, woman, because

I can't understand it."

"I'm yours, Dallas Fontaine. For always. We walk this path *together*. We fight this battle *together*. We win this war *together*."

As if he had no control of his body, tears streamed from his eyes. Unable to resist a second longer, he kissed her—slow and gentle, fast and hard. Exactly how she liked it.

Forcing himself to pull away, he rested his forehead on hers. "I'm so, so sorry for pushing you away. I didn't want you to be burdened. I still don't. But I'm not sure I can make it through this without you, baby. Will you forgive me for ever believing I could—"

"I already have. I'm don't care about the past, Dallas. I'm only looking toward the future. Our future."

"And what do you see in our future?"

"I see you completely cancer-free."

"I like that. What else do you see?"

Rana wrapped her arms around him even tighter. "I see both of us happier than we've ever been in our entire lives."

Dallas smiled. "Keep going."

"I see you coaching me in the labor and delivery room in about seven months. I see—"

Dallas jerked back urgently and eyed her. "*Whoa*! Coaching you in the labor and delivery room in about seven months?" His brow arched. "What does that mean?"

Rana bit at the corner of her lip. "It seems

your soldiers did a little damage, after all."

Dallas's pulse kicked up several notches. "Are you...? Are we...?"

Tears clouded Rana's eyes. She nodded and smiled. "Yes."

"You're pregnant?" he asked for clarification. "Like really, really pregnant?"

"Very pregnant. So you see, Mr. Fontaine, you have no choice but to kick cancer's ass. Our unborn child is counting on it. I'm counting on it."

Choked up with emotion, all Dallas could do was nod dumbly, more tears escaping from his eyes.

Rana cradled his face, wiping the wetness from his cheeks. "You're a good man, Dallas Fontaine. And I love you insanely. And our child will love you because you're going to be one hell of a father."

Dallas lowered to his knees and kissed Rana's stomach what seemed like a thousand times. Tilting his head, he said, "I would die for you, woman. I would die for our child."

Rana dragged a hand down the side of his face. "I know you would. But live for us instead."

He intended to. "You're my miracle, Rana Lassiter. My beautiful miracle. And I'm going to love you until my very last breath."

EPILOGUE

Six Months Later…

Rana wasn't sure whether or not Dallas was actually asleep or just pretending to be, until she heard his light snores. How in the heck could he sleep when tomorrow was such an important day. They would finally get the results of his PET/CT scans.

She inhaled a deep breath and released it slowly, forcing her nerves to calm. *Everything will turn out okay. It has to.* Dallas had endured so much these past few months. Though he was going through his own storm, he never once ignored her. Every OB appointment, he had been there. When her feet swelled, he had rubbed them. Through it all, he had still made her his priority.

Her eyes drifted heavenward. *God, please.*

When her bottom lip trembled, she inched from the bed, wobbled across the room and out onto the balcony. The crisp, chilly air jarred her, but she didn't retreat back inside. Pregnancy kept her piping hot, so the frigid air felt good. Closing her eyes briefly, she drew in a deep cleansing breath.

The full moon lit the dramatic landscape below. The star-filled sky was as clear as she'd ever seen it during her extended stay here at the Fontaine Estate. When Dallas draped a blanket over her shoulders, it startled her, but his strong arms wrapping around her had a calming effect. He rested a hand on her protruding belly and made slow, gentle circles.

"You should be resting, momma," he whispered in her ear, then kissed her lobe.

"Your son won't let me sleep," she offered as an excuse, reclining her head back on his chest. "He's persistent just like his father."

They stood in silence a long time, each lost in their own thoughts.

Dallas's arms tightened around her. "I'm scared, Rana."

Hearing this tugged at her heartstrings, but she couldn't lie. "So am I. But whatever Dr. Newell says tomorrow, know that I will be by your side every step of the way."

He kissed the back of her head. "I know. That's what keeps me going. You and my precious boy."

Several hours later, Rana, Dallas, Denver, and Mrs. Fontaine sat in Dr. Newell's office. Harmen had made up an excuse as to why he couldn't join them; but truthfully, Rana knew he was afraid of whatever news would be delivered. She could see it in his eyes. The man clearly loved Dallas and Denver like his own sons.

Rubbing her belly helped to calm her nerves, but she was surprised her shirt hadn't caught fire from the friction. Dallas captured the offending hand, and Mrs. Fontaine claimed the other and covered it with both hers.

"Relax," Mrs. Fontaine said, rubbing the back

of her hand. "We can't have you going into labor early."

Burning a hole in the carpet, Denver struck the palm of his hand with his fist. "What's taking him so long? He knows—"

Before Denver could finish his thought, the office door opened and Dr. Newell peeped inside. Several sets of inquisitive eyes ogled the man. His stern facial expression gave nothing away. However, in Rana's mind, it was the look of doom.

"Dallas, may I speak with you in the hallway for a moment? Privately."

Oh, God. A fear, unlike anything Rana had ever experienced, flooded her, and she nearly drowned from the effects. Her chest tightened and the air in the room thickened. Why would he need to see Dallas alone? *It's bad news. I know it.*

As if their unborn child could sense his mother's torment, he started turning somersaults in her stomach. *Calm down, baby boy.* For the sake of their child, she decided to take her own advice.

Dallas leaned over and kissed her gently on the lips, then rested his forehead against hers for a moment. "I love you."

Rana's eyes stung with unreleased tears. It was all she could do to keep them from pouring from her eyes. "I love you, too, my knight in shining armor."

A second later, he stood and followed Dr. Newell out. The second the office door clicked shut, Rana broke down. Mrs. Fontaine—a wall of pure strength—rubbed her back. "I'm sorry," Rana said. "I'm sorry," she repeated, wiping at her eyes.

Denver passed her several tissues, then dropped into the chair Dallas had occupied, rested his elbows on his knees and hung his head. Rana rubbed his back. They all had to be strong for one another.

"We'll get through this together," said Mrs. Fontaine. "We'll hire the most renowned specialist in the field. This bastard can't have my son, too."

For the first time, Rana heard a tremble in Mrs. Fontaine's voice. She imagined how hard this must have been for her. Yet, she kept it together, comforting everyone around her. Denver moved to his mother and wrapped her in his arms. It was the most beautiful sight Rana had seen in a long time.

A loud *ding* sounded causing all three of them to flinch.

Mrs. Fontaine rested a hand on her chest. "My, Lord. What was that?"

When several more dings sounded, Denver hurried to the door, eased it open and peeped out. A second later, he performed a single loud clap, then looked back at them. Rana and Mrs. Fontaine crossed the room.

"What is—" Rana stopped abruptly, spotting Dallas standing next to the gold bell attached to the wall. Slapping her hand over her mouth, her eyes clouded with tears.

"Thank, God," Mrs. Fontaine said. "Oh, thank you, God."

Dallas approached Rana and rested his forehead against hers. "We did it, baby. I'm cancer-free. We did it." Tears streamed down his face. "We kicked cancer's ass."

Rana sobbed. "*You* did it."

"Not without you," he said, kissing her tears away. "I couldn't have done it without you."

The following weekend, Mrs. Fontaine insisted on throwing Dallas a gathering to celebrate. A small group—or what Mrs. Fontaine deemed a small group—of family and friends gathered inside the Four Seasons ballroom. Just as to be expected, Mrs. Fontaine hadn't spared any expense in the lavishly decorated space.

Fancy gold and cream linens covered the two rows of rectangular tables. Hundreds of candles ran down the center of the tables and were scattered about the room. Several table-top trees draped with strings of sparkling crystals served as centerpieces. To say it was breathtaking would have been an understatement.

Rana was overjoyed to have her sisters present. Though they'd talked almost every night since she'd been in D.C., it felt like an eternity since she'd seen them. Everyone she loved under one roof. Life couldn't have gotten any better.

She sought Dallas in the crowd, spotting him chatting with several of his cousins and Nico. As if he could sense her gaze on him, their eyes locked. When he winked, her heart fluttered. *Thank you, God*.

A short time later, Dallas tapped a knife against the side of a glass. "May I have your attention, please." Once all eyes fixed in his direction, he continued. "I just wanted to take a moment to thank each and every one of you for being here tonight. Tonight is an incredibly special night for me." He paused. "It has been a trying past few months, but I got through it. And here I stand, cancer-free."

The room erupted into cheers, claps, and words of encouragement.

"Mom…thank you. For the encouragement. For the gentle hand. For the sunsets."

Mrs. Fontaine dabbed at her eyes. "You're welcome, son."

"Harmen," Dallas continued, "you tolerated me when I was intolerable. Thank you for the light, the listening ear and the swift kick in the as—butt."

Chuckles rolled through the room. Rana's heart melted when Harmen rubbed at his eyes, too choked up to speak.

"Denver. Baby brother, I owe you…everything. You saved me from making the biggest mistake of my life. *Thank you. Thank you*. I love you, man. I love all of you."

"We love you, too, bro. And you know I'll always have your back," Denver said.

Denver grinned so wide Rana was sure the corners of his mouth would split. Dallas moved through the crowd until he stood directly in front of her. She had no doubt he was about to say something that would make her cry. Which wouldn't be hard to do, thanks to pregnancy hormones.

"Rana Lassiter," he said.

"Dallas Fontaine."

Dallas smiled, then blew a breath. "Where do I begin?" He studied her for a moment. "Woman, you gave me the will to live. Do you know how powerful that is? To give another human being the will to live. You did that, baby." His voice cracked. "You loved me back to life."

Sounds of endearment came from the crowd. Overwhelmed by Dallas's words, tears streamed down Rana's face. The lump of emotion lodged in her throat kept her from speaking.

Dallas swiped his thumb across her cheeks. "There are no words strong enough to describe the way I feel about you." He lowered his head and pinched the bridge of his nose. "For the record, I never cried before meeting this woman."

The room filled with laughter.

Taking a deep breath, he continued, "You've made me laugh, *made me cry*, made me fight. You've given me so much to live for." He rubbed her stomach. "So much. Now, I want to give you something."

When Dallas lowered to one knee, Rana gasped, then slapped her hand over her mouth. Her heart pounded against her chest.

"Yes!" Gadiya said behind her.

More laughter penetrated the room.

Dallas removed a ring box from his pocket and popped it open. Rana's eyes widened at the size of the square-cut diamond. Five carats, easily. Diamonds made up the band, and the entire piece sparkled insanely under the overhead lighting.

"Rana Lassiter, the first time I laid eyes on you, I knew. I love you with every ounce of my being. I want to spend my life loving you. Will you marry me?"

Her hand fell. "Yes! Yes!" she repeated. "A thousand times, yes."

Dallas slid the ring on her finger, then came to his feet. Resting his forehead against hers, he said, "Marry me right now."

Her brow furrowed. "Marry you right now?"

He nodded. "Tonight's not just for me, Rana. It's for us. Our wedding night."

"You planned a surprise wedding?"

Dallas wiped more tears from her face. "Yes. With a little help from my mother and your sisters."

Rana eyed Gadiya and Sadona, who were both gushing. "I can't believe you two kept this from me." She waved a fist in their direction. Turning back to Dallas, she said, "A surprise wedding?"

"Only if you want it, baby."

Her lips curled. "I do."

A half hour later, they were introduced as Mr. and Mrs. Dallas Fontaine.

"I'm going to make you the happiest woman in the world, Mrs. Fontaine."

"You already have, Mr. Fontaine."

THE END

ABOUT THE AUTHOR

By day, Joy Avery works as a customer service assistant. By night, the North Carolina native travels to imaginary worlds—creating characters whose romantic journeys invariably end happily ever after.

Since she was a young girl growing up in Garner, Joy knew she wanted to write. Stumbling onto romance novels, she discovered her passion for love stories. Instantly, she knew these were the type stories she wanted to pen.

Real characters. Real journeys. Real good love is what you'll find in a Joy Avery romance.

Joy is married with one child. When not writing, she enjoys reading, cake decorating, pretending to expertly play the piano, driving her husband insane, and playing with her dog.

Joy is a member of Romance Writers of America and Heart of Carolina Romance Writers.

ALSO BY JOY AVERY

Smoke in the Citi
His Until Sunrise
Cupid's Error-a novella
His Ultimate Desire
One Delight Night
A Gentleman's Agreement
The Night Before Christian
Another Man's Treasure
Never
Maybe
Always

Harlequin Kimani Romance Titles

In the Market for Love
Soaring on Love
Campaign for His Heart

WHERE YOU CAN FIND ME

WWW.JOYAVERY.COM
FACEBOOK.COM/AUTHORJOYAVERY
TWITTER.COM/AUTHORJOYAVERY
INSTAGRAM.COM/AUTHORJOYAVERY
PINTEREST.COM/AUTHORJOYAVERY
AUTHORJOYAVERY@GMAIL.COM

To stay in the know, click visit my website to sign up for my newsletter *WINGS OF LOVE NEWSLETTER*.

Be sure to follow me on:

AMAZON
BOOKBUB

Made in the USA
Columbia, SC
04 December 2020

26327786R00105